INITIATION

PAGAN EYES, BOOK 1

BY
RAYNA NOIRE

INITIATION

Rayna Noire

Copyright © 2013

Print Edition

CHAPTER ONE

NANA HOBBLED INTO the living room, dragging her left leg behind her, waving the evening newspaper. Red-faced and out of breath, she drew everyone's attention. Mother ran over to her, wrapping one arm around her and urging her to sit down.

"Please, Mama, you must calm down. It's not good for your heart."

Father nodded from his place in the kitchen doorway, drying a plate. Leah's brother, Ethan, watched his grandmother with an expectant expression and drawn breath, probably certain she'd fall to the floor, as she'd only a couple of months before. Luckily, they all lived together. She'd never have survived the stroke on her own. The doctor had instructed them to keep her calm, but often Nana demonstrated the high drama associated with a teenage girl.

Leah stood up and walked over to her grandmother, taking the newspaper from her hand. "What is it, Nana?"

Her brother announced from his spot on the couch, "It's the cyber-bullying article on the front page. I've no worries, Nana. No one bullies me." Ethan pushed up his sleeve and clenched his fist to display a meager bicep, though probably more than most ten-year-olds could lay claim to.

A smile crossed the woman's lined face. "No, sweetheart, no, this is much worse."

Leah's mother, Maura, managed to get Nana to sit in a chair with some difficulty, since only one leg worked right. Leah looked away. It reminded her of the time she'd watched a three-legged dog lie down. The dog never acted like it minded, but it still made her feel bad watching it.

Crouching beside the chair, her mother took Nana's hand. "Tell me, tell us."

Pointing with one hand to Leah, who still clutched the newspaper, she commanded, "Read it to them. Let them know the barbarians still exist. There's no justice, no fairness, no equal rights, and no protection." Her voice became louder and stronger with each word. Her body shook as she half rose from the chair.

Mother cut her eyes meaningfully at her husband, who nodded at Leah, who paged through the paper.

Leah searched for what could be upsetting her grandmother. "Lead story is local boy signing with the NFL." Both her father and mother shook their heads no. She kept paging through the paper. "A huge storm is predicted for the Northeast?"

Grandmother waved her hand in a circle to keep going.

"Ah." She knew that wasn't the right story, but what could it be? On the back page of the front section near the fold was a small article. She knew instinctively it was the one her grandmother meant. "Yesterday, in Papua, New Guinea, a twenty-year-old woman accused of being a witch was burned alive. The young widow and mother left two small children behind."

Her grandmother shook off her daughter's hand. Stabbing the air with an emphatic index finger, she crowed, "See? See? They're at it again." Her dark eyes darted around the room to make sure she'd everyone's attention. "That poor girl. What was her crime, really?"

Maura sighed. "Just twenty, so young. Could be she was too pretty and attracted a married man's eye. Calling her a witch is always a good way to get rid of her. It worked countless times before."

Her father laid down the plate and towel and walked into the living room to join the conversation. He sat down on the couch on the other side of Ethan. "Something happened in their village. Chickens weren't laying or a goat died. It's always easier to blame it on the evil eye or a hex, than accept it for what it is. Just life, luck, usually both. People always seem to believe life owes them more than they deserve. The only way to rationalize not getting it is to blame someone for blocking it."

Ethan joined in. "Just like calling someone a cheat, a liar, or even a bully."

"In a way," Maura agreed. "But not exactly. People don't feel it is okay to kill people for telling a lie or even being accused of telling a lie. The hatred goes bone deep, associated with fear and helplessness. Even the simple fact she'd no man to stand for her would be enough to persecute her."

Leah stood, silent, thinking that only a few years separated her from the young woman burned alive. Yesterday, her history teacher, Miss Santiago, had grown as animated as Nana talking about human slavery in the US. Her voice had become shrill as she'd spoken of undocumented workers not receiving any pay for their work and being kept in unheated garages, treated no better than animals. After class, the popular girls, Lauren, Brianna, and Alexis, had joked about Miss Santiago's behavior, even pretending to be her, waving their arms and bugging out their eyes, spitting out the words. The other students had enjoyed their performance. Leah hadn't. Besides being mean, she'd had no reason to appease the girls. She already knew she was on their short list.

Yeah, she knew her teacher had gone overboard, but she knew without having it spelled out that it was personal. Often Leah knew things without words, just as she knew someone close to Miss Santiago had died under such conditions. Leah knew all about taking things personally. A woman burned as a witch was personal for her family. How could it not be when her entire family followed the old ways?

Her family circled her grandmother, trying to calm her down without much success. Leah leaned back against the wall the offending newspaper still in her hand, she wanted to throw it to the ground and flee. An image took shape in her mind. It was dark, most likely night. The sound of running, yelling, and then screaming, a long prolonged scream as if whoever uttered it felt absolute terror. A spark charged the night, then caught fire and became a flame, growing into an orb of light. It illuminated sweaty, dark faces with feverish eyes and determined countenances. Two strong men stripped to the waist held a woman between them. Her long hair covered her face as she struggled.

Off to the side, a chair sat on a dais. An almost skeletal man sat there, garbed in a long robe. His lips quirked up as the men wrestled the woman, who wore a coarse, shapeless gown, to a standstill in front of him. A brutal push shoved her to her knees. The sound of weeping almost broke Leah's heart. She was watching what had happened in New Guinea only days before.

No doubt, the man on the dais had caused this woman to be in such a situation. The crying continued as the man ordered. "Let me look on the face of the witch." The surrounding crowd hissed and murmured. Most threw their hands in front of their faces or looked away as if looking at the woman's face might hurt them. She couldn't. The woman deserved her respect. One guard grabbed her long dark hair and yanked, snapping her head up. Despite the tears glistening on her skin, her expression was defiant. Her face was familiar. It should have been, since she saw it every morning in the mirror as she brushed her hair.

HER LEGS, MORE rubberlike than bone and muscle, slid out from under her, landing her on the floor. What did it mean? Nana used to tell her the visions she received were similar to a tornado watch. It didn't necessarily mean the vision would happen, but it was best to get ready for it in case it did. Most of her visions included small things, such as being ridiculed by Lauren and Brianna or failing an algebra test, or slipping on the ice and losing two teeth. It all had happened, except the teeth. Whenever she saw anything glistening like ice, she avoided it, keeping her teeth intact so far.

The image of the man on the dais chilled her, unlike any amount of teeth-cracking ice could. The clothes she wore, the way the man spoke, none of it made sense. Her mother's voice broke into her daze.

"Leah, what are you doing? Try to be of some help, will you? Go get your grandmother a glass of water. Ethan, go get Nana's protection heart charm from the box in her bedroom."

Pushing up to her knees, she watched her brother scamper out of the room to retrieve the charm. Her mother threw her an irritated look, probably because she was still sitting there. Standing, she walked to the kitchen, but she could hear them talking. Her grandmother's shrill voice carried.

"Maura." Her voice had an imperious tone that defied her fragile appearance. "Be gentle with your daughter. Soon, she will be called on to make the ultimate sacrifice."

The ultimate sacrifice? The water splashed over the glass rim as she continued to hold it under the faucet, not seeing it but instead the glee in the man's face who'd called her a witch. She truly hoped her grandmother didn't expect her to become a burnt offering.

Turning off the faucet, she tipped the glass to pour out the excess water. Taking a dishtowel, she dried the glass. Nana could trace her ancestry back to Romany gypsies. She claimed this centuries-old bond allowed her to turn the Tarot cards with surprising accuracy for her loyal clients. Leah had doubts about her grandmother's actual ability, though the fact she'd seen the same clients faithfully for years made Leah wonder. Then there were the crystals and charms strewn about the family home, which kept her from inviting classmates over. All she really wanted was just to be another teenage girl obsessed with drama and boys. Well, only the boys part...one boy, Dylan Torres, if she was honest with herself.

As she handed the glass to Nana, their hands touched. Her grandmother's eyes gleamed dark with intelligence. The brief glance conveyed awareness of Leah's inner turmoil. It was the equivalent of kneeling to bury her face against Nana's shoulder, sobbing out her confusion, her fears, and her inappropriate attraction to Dylan, whose father happened to be a Pentecostal minister. A bad thing about the Pentecostals was the fact they actually believed witches existed and shouldn't, rather like cockroaches.

As her grandmother's fingers touched hers, the look, the touch, and the sudden knowledge that her legacy was to never be a normal girl caused her heart to plummet. No matter what excuses she might make for Nana's uncanny ability, she recognized Nana was never wrong.

Curious why so many well-heeled ladies would come month after month to have her grandmother tell their fortunes, she'd asked. Nana's answer had implied that knowing helped people shape their destiny and relieved stress. Seeing herself about to be burned at the stake didn't make her feel less stressed. Rather, just the opposite.

✦   ✦   ✦

NANA EVENTUALLY CALMED down. Adam, Leah's father, talked his determined mother-in-law out of calling the news organizations. Any negative attention might influence her father's engineering job. Nana understood this on one hand, but on another, she didn't since she chose not to hide what she was. Her grandmother had as much bravado as a drag queen in full costume demonstrating for marriage equality. There was a good chance she was pecking out a letter to the editor on her old typewriter. Leah had noticed a few of the letters in the papers, signed as Pagan Philosopher, had sounded exactly like Nana in full rant.

Her father had never mentioned the letters, which meant he'dn't seen them or had realized he could exercise no control over his mother-in-law. For years, the family had maintained a careful balance trying to please both extended families. Father's family was ultra-religious and had named their children Adam and Eve, somehow missing the incestuous connotation in the pairing. Everything that was part of the secular world was not only evil, but also forbidden. How he and her mother had ended up together appeared to be an unfathomable question. It could have been the lure of the forbidden, but more likely, it had started out as lust. Her father never would put it so bluntly, but she'd seen the pictures of them together in college. No doubt, many men had craved her mother's dark, almost foreign, beauty, but she'd chosen instead the shy, short, bespectacled engineering student.

Her mother's reasoning for their romance was he accepted her the way she was. It would be great if someone accepted Leah for who she was. She peered at her own image in the mirror, complete with a disbelieving smirk. It indicated her non-belief of her father's total acceptance of her mother. Nana had chided her son-in-law on numerous occasions for keeping quiet about their religious beliefs. Inquiries from his parents asking if they'd been to church that week were usually appeased by saying they had. He intentionally forgot to mention their services took place on a farm ten miles out of town, often under the light of a full moon. Her father had decided to follow the old ways to humor his wife, but Leah suspected it was mainly to get his mother-in-law off his back.

Setting her alarm clock for the school day, she noted five hours had passed since the news meltdown. Theodora, her cat, jumped on the bed, kneading the pillow with her paws as if preparing it. Leah knew the feline was making her own bed. Grabbing another pillow from the floor, she placed it on the bed. Dropping her clothes on the floor, she climbed between the cool sheets. Locking her hands behind her head, she stared at the ceiling, thinking about her parents' relationship. Her parents got along better than most. Her family life was unusual in that she'd both original parents living in the same house. Still, she wanted more than what they had, something stronger, bolder, something void of the timidity her father demonstrated in hiding from his parents that Maura was a witch, as was her grandmother.

No doubt, they had figured out Esmeralda Hare was a bit different, loving to play up the image of the carnival fortune-teller with flowing skirts, too much jewelry, and always wishing everyone a blessed day or merry meet again. The word most commonly used for Nana was "colorful." Nora, Leah's older sister, had confided once she'd overheard an argument between their parents over her father never telling his parents they didn't celebrate Christmas or Easter. None of the kids had cared because they'd enjoyed the Easter baskets and Christmas presents given to them by their grandparents.

Grandfather had retired from the ministry the same time his wife had divorced him. Instead of warning everyone to stay on the straight and narrow, he'd donned tie-dyed shirts, made home-brewed beer, and attended the concerts of aging rock stars. Nora had pointed out that Grandfather would accept the family's religion since he'd changed so much on his own. Of course, their father chose to say nothing. As much as Leah loved her father, she acknowledged, if only to herself, most of his actions were motivated out of fear of being different or that people might not like him. It wasn't so much that he accepted mother just how she was, but rather she accepted him with his fears, worries, and rules, able to see past everything to the caring man inside.

Scratching Theodora's head, she confided to the cat, "I won't be like that. I'm who I'm. It doesn't matter what people think."

The feline blinked her eyes as if commenting on the bold statement. Leah sighed. "You're right. I know. For all my brave words, I'm no better than my father." Balling up her fist, she pounded her pillow in disgust. "Coward, that's all I'm."

Threading her fingers under Theo's heavy body, she cradled the cat. The cat let out a few plaintive mews, but resigned herself to the cuddling, even to the point of purring. "Theodora, what am I to do? I know I'm a fraud. I talk of nothing of consequence to Dylan. Questions about homework, reactions to pop quizzes, and comments on the weather are another way to spell lame. Brianna, at least, flirts with him."

The popular blonde's flirtatious banter always seemed to switch on whenever she was near a cute guy. It didn't matter that her boyfriend, Marcus, was a senior football player who'd scored scholarships at six colleges. Could be Brianna was looking for a replacement, not that she'd consider Dylan. He was too small a deal for her, too young, not popular enough. His father was a minister, which made him the male equivalent to poison ivy. Brianna only flirted with him because Leah liked him. Worse, she'd confessed to liking Dylan in a brief spate of time when she and Brianna had been friends.

Looking back, she wondered if it had been some elaborate scheme to get information. No doubt, Brianna had relayed to Dylan that Leah had a serious crush on him. If it bothered him too much, he could stop talking to her. Then again, if he did like her, he could ask her out, which he'd'nt. The third option was Brianna hadn't told him or he'd chosen not to believe her. If it were the last, then he'd showed more sense than Leah had.

"I can see your light on," her mother called through the locked door.

Leah clapped her hands, turning the light off. As a kid, she'd been so enamored of the clapper lamp that her parents had bought her one. Most people would label it hokey, but she still liked it.

"Good girl," her mother admonished, before tacking on, "Love you."

"Love you, too, Mom," she called back, closing her eyes, easing into sleep. Tomorrow would be another day, just like so many others. The image of the man in the throne-like chair flickered into her weary mind. Sitting up, she shook her head to shake the offending image out. "I refuse to dream about him. I'll think of something pleasant, such as Dylan asking me to the homecoming dance."

Lying back down, she let her eyelids flick closed. Maybe Dylan didn't dance. She'd heard some of those religions had rules against it. Something about if people danced, they'd end up having sex like rabbits. As she drifted off to sleep, her last thought was she couldn't remember ever seeing a dancing rabbit.

✧   ✧   ✧

THE SMELL STRUCK her first. The acrid, smelly odor reminded her of her fourth-grade field trip to a pioneer village. The candle maker had intrigued her by dipping wicks in what she'd assumed was wax until the woman explained it was made of animal fat from butchered animals. That's what it smelled like, along with the campfire aroma of burning wood.

In the misty night sky, a clouded crescent moon shed meager light on the surroundings. Turning slowly she examined the primitive thatched hut behind her. In the small front garden, a split log supported by two stumps served as a bench. An oaken bucket sat by a door that flew open. An elderly woman hobbled out, dressed in a black cloak. The woman reminded Leah of her grandmother, but instead of a look of fierce determination, terror pulled her face into an anxious mask. Reaching Leah, she tugged on her clothes, pushing her toward the woods. "Flee, flee, they come. Smell the torches." The woman pointed to a path winding toward the east.

A dim glow was coming from that direction, along with the sounds of voices and snapping branches as dozens of feet marched in their direction. An overwhelming desire to run after the unknown woman came over her. Another part of her wanted to see who was coming down the path. It was only a dream, right? People couldn't be hurt in a dream, or could they? She struggled to remember what her psychology teacher, Mr. Schaeffer, had said. He'd said either people couldn't be hurt by their fears or your fears could kill you by bringing on cardiac arrest.

A few men came into view, burly men garbed in shapeless garments, with wild hair and ragged beards. Held high, flickering torches illuminating a small circle around them. One held a curved knife, reminiscent of the scythe the grim reaper carried. It didn't bode well. One of the men spotted her, yelled, "Witch!" and charged her way. It was a definite bad sign, causing her to sprint toward the woods in the same direction as the old woman. Sticks, rocks, and briars pierced her feet, reminding her of her shoeless state. At home, she excelled in cross-country, but she'd shoes, sunlight, and a feel for the course with no angry villagers behind her. The running men drew closer. Leah stumbled over a tree root, wasting precious time.

"Here, over here." The voice came from overhead. Staring up into the canopy of leaves, she saw a small hand motioning to her. Of course, hide in the trees. Why didn't she think of that? Grabbing the lowest limb, she pulled herself into the leafy covering. In the dark, she felt for the branches, climbing higher. Eventually she grabbed an ankle or calf, and received a hand up for her trouble, helping her climb higher.

Good Goddess, how many people were in this tree? She held her breath as the light and noise came closer. The men below argued about which way to go, while a woman waded in with her opinion. "Samuel, let the witch get away. Mayhap he uses the witch for his own purposes."

One of the front-runners denied the accusations. "Martha seeks to harm my name, because I did not plight my troth with her."

The argument moved on a little farther away from the tree. Leah exhaled in a whoosh, thanking the stars for the scorned woman and lack of dogs. As if hearing her silent prayer, a long canine bay rent the air.

More footsteps ran underneath their tree, where there was some minor disagreement about which way to go, then they ran after the previous party. The sound of her heart was so loud in her ears she couldn't believe her pursuers hadn't heard it. The barking dog came closer, along with the sound of its handler.

"Ar-roo, Ar-roo." The dog sounded close, very close. Its nails scratching at her tree stopped Leah's heart. Stupid canine. She was history. She was ready to drop out of the tree and give herself up when a hand touched her and stopped her in the dark. A single word sounded in her ear. "Wait."

Two villagers stood under the tree, arguing. "Pull the hound off the tree. You will anger the tree spirits. Misfortune will befall us entering the forest at night."

"Umfrey, still your wild speech. You speak of the old ways. We're now all Christians by order of the king. Such talk will cause the witch hunters to take you up."

"I tell you this, Collin. A decree does not make the tree spirits, the fairies, the mysterious lights in the woods cease to be. Do you think they bow to kings?"

The dog's protest about the lack of interest in his treed prey caused Leah's heart to slow a tiny bit, but not return to normal. Crouched in the tree, similar to blackbirds on the line, she waited with the still unseen others.

"Morn is coming, and the field needs plowing. Umfrey, I will return, not because of your fears of tree fairies and what not, but because I've land to attend to."

"Good call. Your Mary may have some porridge simmering over the fire."

She listened to them move away. The staying hand remained on her *arm. They all crouched in the tree for what seemed like hours as they waited for each group of witch hunters to pass by them. Dawn colored the sky with a pink glow, giving way to the sun's rays.*

Finally, the hand released Leah's arm. They dropped out of the tree, one by one, the old crone in the black cloak, a young woman a bit older than herself but not by much, and a man, which surprised her. "I didn't think they took men as witches." She covered her mouth with her hand, realizing she'd spoken the words aloud.

The young woman stared at her, "What manner of speech is this?"

Before she could answer, the weathered-looking man chose to answer her inquiry. "They take whoever has trespassed against the village elders in some form or manner. My sin is I accused the miller of using unfair scales. People like Old Margaret, who has no one to stand for her, also are taken."

Turning to the young woman, Leah touched her own chest with her hand. "My speech is different because I'm from America."

"A Mer Rica." The young woman tried to sound out the name. "Strange, I never heard talk of such a place. My name is Sabina."

"Leah," she answered, pointing to herself.

Sabina cocked her head at her slightly, "Is that your real name or your witch name? It is best you do not speak your Christian name."

Her witch name? Her grandmother had insisted on giving her the witch name Raven, but she never used it. "I assume Sabina is your witch name."

Sabina bobbed her head as if the whole discussion was a no-brainer. "It is and isn't. I didn't have a witch name to begin with, but since we will go to a new town, I will need a new name. Sabina it is. Witches only give out their false name to each other else it will be spoken under the pain of torture."

It made sense. She remembered something about that when Nana had made her watch one of those online videos about the Burning Times, full of grainy black-and-white illustrations of people being tortured in myriad of ways. *Guilty or innocent, somehow the people had always ended up dead.*

Margaret started walking in the direction of her house. The man grabbed her arm. "No, someone will wait at the cottage for your return."

The old woman struggled in his grasp. "I must save Odo."

"Odo is a creature of the wild. He can take care of himself better than you," the man insisted, turning the woman to walk deeper into the woods.

A whoosh and the sound of crackling caused them all to turn in the direction of Old Margaret's house. A thick plume of smoke filled the air, darkening the morning sky. The old woman cried out, "That is all I have!" and shook in the man's half embrace.

Sabina stepped forward to touch the woman's cheek, wet with tears. "You have life, Margaret. Once the witch hunters come, you can never return home."

Sorrow swept over Leah for the weeping devastated woman. Margaret raised her head to glare at Leah. Pulling herself out of comforting arms, she pointed one bony finger at Leah. "You're the reason they came. If I had not found you in the forest and took you and gave you succor, I would have my home and my beloved Odo."

Found her in the forest? At least that explained how she'd ended up here, but not really. "I'm sorry. I did not mean to hurt you or Odo."

"Margaret," the man inserted. "You're speaking out of your loss. It was only a matter of time before they came for each of us. We all knew it. Why else did we create witch names or assemble our dark clothing so we can vanish into the night? We do not call ourselves witches. We may not worship the new god or practice the old ways to ensure a good crop, but that does not make us evil, or witches. Still, once others call us witches, we have to prepare."

Leah wanted to protest that witches weren't evil, but she listened and considered the trio. The man served as a sort of shepherd, as he managed to get everyone back on the trail through the woods. He nodded to Leah. "You *can call me Henry."*

Leah nodded to him, well aware that Henry probably wasn't his name. "Thanks. This is a new place for me, and I appreciate your help."

Henry nodded and gestured to the path ahead. "Make haste. Many have chores to do. Most fear the monks more who travel to villages stirring up suspicions with their talk of witches and intercourse with the devil. They will head back into the woods in search of people they can label witches. Their sins might have been lingering in the woods too long or picking herbs for a disorder instead of calling on a physician. I heard an entire town in Germany was taken up as witches, the children, and priests, too. The blood lust is on them, making me wonder if there will be any people left to populate the earth."

Leah shuddered. Hearing or reading about the Burning Times was something entirely different from walking through the woods with people accused of being witches. Not a good different, either. She preferred the distance accompanying a span of centuries. Still, there had to be a reason behind this. These dreams were more realistic than anything she'd dreamt before. Was the universe speaking to her? Was this something she should understand? In a way similar to her father, she never spoke about her faith. Could be she was having a crisis of faith.

"Sabina, I was wondering what happened to people who practice the old ways."

"Same thing," the woman replied matter-of-factly. "We're all people in the way of the newest religion, government, or what comes down the road. No place for differences. Everyone has to be the same. Is that the practice where you come from?"

Just before falling asleep, she'd wondered the same thing. "I thought it was, but not as bad here. Being different or practicing the old ways might keep me from getting a date I might want or hanging out with the popular kids, but I doubt our house would get burned down."

Sabina regarded her oddly. "What is a date or hanging out? Why are these things important?"

Good question. How did she explain dating, especially if these people participated in the practice of arranged marriages? She searched for a way to explain, but a beeping interrupted her explanation.

Leah blinked. Dawn's light peeked through her blinds, dappling her walls. Theodora meowed in her ear, reminding her breakfast, at least hers, was eminent. A loud trio of knocks rattled her door.

Ethan yelled, "Are you awake? Mom said to make sure you were awake so you wouldn't be late to school."

"I'm awake! I'm awake." She gently pushed Theo off her chest to sit up. Placing her bare feet on the floor, she cataloged everything familiar. Yes, she was home. The woods were just a dream.

CHAPTER TWO

LEAH RUSHED TO pull on her school uniform of monogrammed polo and khaki pants. The good thing about uniforms was there was no time lost deciding what to wear. It also eliminated another potential target for the mean girls. A hairbrush failed to coerce her hair into some sort of order. Biting her bottom lip, she tried to clear her mind from her troubling dreams.

Opening her door, she peered down the hallway, checking the possibility of scooting into the bathroom. The closed door wasn't what she wanted to see. Great. A family of five sharing one bathroom made for early-morning headaches. Only a few months ago, before her older sister, Nora, headed off to college, it had been worse. Ethan's vocalizing reached her ears. Her bladder was ready to burst, while her baby brother used the bathroom as his own personal sound booth.

Tired of waiting hammered on the bathroom door. "C'mon, other people need to use the bathroom." Her brother grumbled on the other side of the door but did not open it.

Her mother opened her bedroom door while still buttoning her own white uniform. "Kids, enough, too much noise."

"Mom." Leah turned to complain about her brother, who suddenly opened the door.

Ethan flashed a large grin and indicated the bathroom with a swooping flourish, "My lady, your bathroom awaits."

Her mother glared at Leah as if she'd caused the problem. Pushing past her brother, she slammed the door. Staring into the mirror, she leaned on the sink. Dark circles drew attention to her eyes, making her resemble a silent-movie actress. Today would be a makeup day. Just as well. Wearing makeup often felt like she wore a mask, pretending to be someone she wasn't. Smoothing on cover-up, she considered the distance makeup put between her and the next person. Most of her life she'd rejected primping, but not so much now.

Curling her eyelashes, she wondered who influenced her behavior more, Dylan or the mean girl trio of Brianna, Alexis, and Lauren. She wanted to look nice for Dylan, but then again she didn't want to attract the attention, either. The three-headed dog of Hades, Cerberus, was the name she'd given to the girls, never aloud, though. Cerberus paid close attention to the other students' appearance, especially the girls, looking for something to heckle. The uniforms protected those who couldn't buy the expensive clothes Cerberus favored out of school. Even a pimple or a wayward booger caught on the tip of someone's nose made the person a minor celebrity in a very bad way.

She swooped up her lashes with black mascara, exacting a fine line between the right amount of makeup and too much. Once previously, her eyeliner had been a little heavy. Alexis had sidled up to her and asked her if she was going Goth. Lauren and Brianna had told a couple of Goth boys she was crushing on them. While smoothing clear lip-gloss over her lips, she wondered how the girls managed to keep their grades up when they spent so much time taunting others. It wouldn't surprised if they blackmailed other students into doing their homework.

At her mother's brisk knock, she opened the door. "Hurry, Leah, if you want a ride to school with your father."

"Yes, Mom," she answered. Riding the bus would be the ultimate slap to her self-esteem. The recognizable yellow school buses bore the nickname Loser Cruisers. Students who could afford to drive did. There was no extra money in their household for more than the aging sedan her father drove. Her mother rode to work with another nurse's aide, while her grandmother walked the few blocks to Madame Zelda's Magick Shoppe. Only Ethan had no issue with riding the school bus.

Her grandmother handed her an apple and lunch as Leah tagged after her father. As she bit into her apple, she heard Nana call after her. "When you come home, Leah, we'll talk."

She almost said about *what?* Since her mouth was full, she chewed instead.

Nana held up her index finger. "You know what I mean. No worries, it can wait until you return."

Her father opened the garage door for her and asked, "Do you know what she is talking about, Trinka?"

Her father's use of his pet name both warmed and embarrassed her. It reminded her of a simpler time when she used to beg her father for trinkets when he'd returned from road trips. She'd often searched through his pockets filled with plastic jewelry, cat-eyed sunglasses, tiny dolls, and candy. It was never good when he used the pet name in public where people could hear him. Leah usually didn't want to explain, believing it made her sound greedy. To keep from answering, she bit into her apple again and shrugged her shoulder as if she were clueless.

No good would come of telling her father of her dreams and visions. As a practical man who grudgingly tolerated Nana's emphatic Pagan ways and accepted his wife's less showy ways, he persevered to be unremarkable and pragmatic. Her television watching or books would merit blame for her dreams. There might have been some truth in such rationale. Still, it was hard to separate the real terror last night from some boring documentary with shaky camera action her grandmother always urged her to watch.

Her father backed out of the garage slowly, looking over his shoulder at the driveway. "How's school?"

His inquiry indicated he'd forgotten his original question, which worked. Unfortunately, he must have read an article or felt some paternal guilt about not connecting to prompt his latest foray into her life. Most of the time, her father acted as if he were adrift in the waves his family created, not that he yelled or bullied, like some fathers. Unlike other dads, he actually lived in the house with them and helped with chores. He'd occasionally flash a smile or slap her on the back when she'd earned some academic award or made the honor roll. Lately, since she always made the honor roll, it no longer merited a special, "Way to go!"

Unlike Stella's father, hers never told her he wished she'd never been born and his life would have been better without kids. How cold was that? Nope, her father loved all his offspring, but his hesitancy about parenting was obvious. His anxiety about saying or doing the wrong thing made her want to reassure him, which made for an unusual relationship. After twenty years of fatherhood, you'd think he'd have loosened up, but this might have been as loose as he would get. Probably late at night, he combed through the Internet looking for an elusive parenting manual, which included diagrams and flow charts. It was better to honor his attempts.

"Not flunking," she said and took another bite of the apple. It wasn't the largest apple in the world, so she might have to make real conversation if she ate too fast.

He chuckled as he turned out of the neighborhood. "I should say not, not with two intelligent parents."

Leah's lips turned down. There, that was the problem. Yes, both her parents were intelligent, but what about her contribution? The work just didn't do itself. The reason she couldn't connect with her father was he saw her as a product of Adam and Maura, as opposed to an individual.

Her gaze flickered to her father, who drove with both hands on the wheel.

Was it harsh of her to judge him? He probably always did as told, never questioning, never rebelling. Leah never wondered if he did drugs when he was younger. She knew the answer was an unequivocal "no." The words popped out before she thought about them. "Dad, did you always follow the rules when you were in school?"

"Yes, as well as I could. Sometimes, there were rules I didn't understand or social pecking order I truly didn't get until I was pecked a few times." He turned his head to glance at her. Oh, he might reveal something of himself. Another reason she felt a tenacious connection with her father. All she knew was his parents had been Sales Reps for Christ, peddling the wonders of religion from both the pulpit and the street corner until his mother had taken up with a visiting evangelist and left. Her desertion had made Grandpa Carpenter transform himself into an aging hippie with talk about meditation, life's journey, and brewing methods. At last, she'd get a glimpse into the secretive man who was her father.

Her lips curved up in satisfaction as she mentally scrolled through all the things she'd always wanted to ask. There were many. A motion at the edge of her vision caught her eye. "Dog!" she screamed, causing her father to swerve, barely missing the small white dog, someone's indulged pet.

His hands gripped the steering wheel with an unnatural ferocity. No doubt, he was internally lecturing himself on what happens when you glance away from the road. It didn't matter that ninety percent of the time there was no one else on Mulholland, a back road to the school. The tension lines around his mouth were obvious, indicating the small window of opportunity to find out more about him had just closed.

Neither of them spoke the rest of the ride. Her father was probably going over everything he could have done differently, a mental debriefing of the near-miss incident. Her thoughts jumped between avoiding Cerberus, seeing Dylan, and wondering about her father. When her grandpa had abruptly turned into this mellow fellow, she'd thought it would allow her own father to relax some, but it hadn't.

How would she feel if suddenly her parents moved to Utah and declared themselves Mormons? The mental picture of herself in a long, unfashionable dress came to mind, along with her father trying to juggle multiple wives. Of course, that was just how Mormons were portrayed on a television show. Mormons were probably about the same as her family, trying to live average lives. People only imagined they were different.

The sprawl of the high school came into view. It was a mishmash of buildings and connecting hallways. Every time the city population went up, they threw up a new wing. There was no organization or planning in the details, which made it close to impossible to get from geometry to civics in the four-minute passing period. The idea was to not allow students time to linger at their lockers or flirt. Flirting was hard when you were jogging through four buildings to get to your next class. Forget talking. Often, she found catching her breath difficult as she sprinted for the open door of her civics class. Mr. Patterson took delight in closing the door and locking it, forcing the tardy students to go to the office for a pass and make the long trek back. Never mind the student returned twenty minutes later, missing a good chunk of the class.

Her father slowed as they approached one of the initial wings. He did her the courtesy of not taking her up to the central drop-off. It allowed Leah the opportunity to slip into the school unnoticed. Some students, but more likely the parent, enjoyed the big goodbye scene where the mother trilled loudly for her darling child to have a wonderful day and learn something as if he were five. Some even forced their child to publicly kiss them. Did those mothers even consider how their behavior made their child the butt of teasing and bullying? She doubted they thought of it. Instead, the handful of parents with an insane need for attention took any attention they could get, even from the handful of slackers who hung around outside the school as long as they could.

Leah exited the car, turned and waved at her father. Overall, he was okay, just a man trying to find his way in a world that constantly shifted on him. Grandpa changing overnight from a hell-and-damnation preacher to a clerk at the local organic market must have taken some getting used to. What Grandpa had morphed into might not even have been the problem, but the change itself.

A few students she barely knew called out greetings, which she answered. Leah never thought of herself as a popular person, never really made the effort to be so. An incident a few months ago in German class had bought her some notoriety and a small cult following.

Jeremy's father had died unexpectedly, which had forced the high school junior to work long hours after school to support his mother and younger siblings. The result was he fell asleep in class. Herr Vaughn never took that well. He would drop books near Jeremy's head, slap, or kick his desk, jolting him awake. He often grumbled loudly about how worthless Jeremy was, causing the other students to giggle nervously, glad not to be on the receiving end of his ire. One day she'd had it.

Ironically, she didn't know Jeremy all that well, even though they'd passed through various grades together. He was a tall, shy boy in desperate need of braces his family couldn't afford. His determination to help support his family told her even more than his appearance. Stella whispered something once about his mother being handicapped or sick as the reason she couldn't support the family. When Herr Vaughn had started in on Jeremy, she'd held up her hand. Yes, held up her hand. She was a rule follower like her father and waited for acknowledgment before speaking.

She'd stood and explained in a few short sentences the train wreck called Jeremy's life of long hours, little sleep, and even less pay working as an assistant manager at a local fast-food restaurant. The smirk on the teacher's face had melted away as he'd considered the sleeping boy. The class had burst into a spontaneous applause that embarrassed her. She'd thought for sure she'd get a write-up for her actions, but she hadn't.

Jeremy had slept through her explanation and the class reaction, which indicated his exhaustion. During the next class, she'd overheard Herr Vaughn tell Jeremy he could sleep in his class, and he would still pass. The story had spread all over the school in two days, making her sort of a giant slayer. A few other teachers had decided to let Jeremy sleep, too.

She noticed Cerberus to her left and nodded to the three. To ignore them would invite their catty remarks. To actually talk to them might result in them ignoring her. She'd decided a head bob worked best. Her folk legend status protected her some, not that she deserved it. Hard to know what had gotten into her, causing her to act in such a way. All she knew was she hated seeing people accused unfairly. Something deep within her had caused her to act without thinking things through.

The buzzer sounded right when she stepped into the classroom. Good thing she'd decided against darting into the bathroom on her way to check her hair. Dylan looked up at her entrance, smiled slightly then looked down at his paper. Her heart tripped. It had to mean something, right? She thought he liked her. Why would he smile at her otherwise? A voice punctured her thoughts and her ear.

"Move it, will ya? You're blocking my opportunity to accumulate the vast stores of knowledge awaiting me."

A skinny male with thick glasses managed to push around her. Great, she'd Dooran to thank for her major humiliation. Slinking to the back of the classroom, she slid into her seat, fighting the desire to open her geometry book and use it to cover her face. Wasn't it enough she was already one year behind in math due to their moving? Most of the other students were younger. Dooran was only a jumped-up ninth-grader after skipping a grade or something, which might explain why he was so obnoxious.

Still, she glanced at the boy who already had his hand up to answer a question the teacher hadn't asked since the equation wasn't on the white board yet. On the first or second day of school, he'd run into the door, thus earning him the nickname "Dooran." Leah wasn't even sure of his real name. Still, with that type of welcome, you'd think he'd stay low, but he didn't. Instead, he rattled off wordy phrases, sounding like someone from a nineteenth-century novel.

Dooran forgotten, her attention drifted up to Dylan, or at least his back. Since everyone wore the same blue polo shirt, you'd think everyone would look the same. That wasn't true. Many girls tried to make statements with jewelry, wildly colored socks or too much makeup, which lasted about one period until Mrs. Collins caught them. Nicknamed "The Enforcer," the petite biology teacher roamed the halls during passing periods on the lookout for uniform breakers. Girls who had unbuttoned their polo one extra button found themselves not only re-buttoning it, but also earning a detention for their daring display. It never did any good to complain against a uniform violation because The Enforcer's word was law.

Leah didn't worry about censure since her own goal was to escape notice. Doing anything extraordinary would get her noticed. She didn't need or want that, especially after their last move. Ironically, her family must have moved around the same time as Jeremy's had, since they'd ended up in the same schools. His move had probably happened because of his father's death. Hers, on the other hand, had happened for reasons she wasn't totally clear about. Her father had made some comment about the neighborhood not being safe, which was odd since they'd moved into an obviously poorer area.

She resumed her study of Dylan's neck. His hair ended in a square cut right above his collar, indicating his desire to stay with dress code. A large freckle punctuated the uniformity of his light skin.

"Ms. Carpenter, paging Ms. Carpenter." The teacher's words caused all those around her to giggle. Leah's eyes jerked up to where her instructor regarded her with a knowing gaze and folded arms. Dooran waved his hand vigorously, trying to catch the math teacher's attention.

Her father always reminded her: When in a difficult position, use your manners and stall. "Yes, sir, could you repeat the question, please?"

The teacher's pointer landed on the whiteboard where three triangles drawn in different-colored markers, he asked, "Which one is acute?"

Good. She knew this one. "Is not the one in the middle, the green one, because it is less than ninety degrees." Feeling cocky, she added, "The red one is obtuse because it is more than ninety degrees, and the third is a right angle because it is ninety degrees."

Instead of looking pleased with her, her instructor looked disgruntled. "Very good, Ms. Carpenter. I will accept that you may have paid attention the first week of class, but how would you compute the area of a triangle?" He nodded in her direction.

What had she done to earn this spotlight? Not paying attention was the culprit. "Multiply the base by the height, and then divide by two."

"Right, moving on." He returned to the board to write something else, which gave Dylan just enough time to turn and wink at her.

He did like her. Aniyah, who sat beside her, nudged her. "Did you see that Dylan Torres winked at me?"

"Oh, he did?" It was the best Leah could come up with. Who had he winked at? Aniyah was cute, friendly, intelligent, and a star athlete. Who wouldn't like her? Slumping in her seat, she decided she was ready to head to English class, where she hadn't have to worry about Dylan crushing on any of the girls sitting next to her. It felt like she'd swallowed a rock, a big one, which managed to lodge in her throat.

✦ ✦ ✦

THE STUDENTS REACTED to the buzzer like a floodgate had opened. They rushed to the doorway, pushing their way into the exterior hallway. Leah hung back, unsure what she wanted to happen. Maybe she could talk to Dylan in the hallway. Then again, he might walk right past her or, worse yet, talk to Aniyah. Before she could make her decision, her math teacher called her name, "Ms. Carpenter, may I have a moment?"

What had she done now? Her feet, feeling the pull of gravity, shuffled toward his desk. "Yes, sir," she answered and made eye contact. Convey sincerity, she coached herself, keeping visual contact.

"Ms. Carpenter," he started, stopped, cracking his knuckles. "You're a very bright student, probably one of the brightest in my class. At this point, you can indulge in your obsession with Mr. Torres and still answer any question I throw at you, but the class speed is about to pick up. The material will be tougher and will require more attention on your part. Do you understand?"

"Yes, sir," she answered as her face heated. Obsession? She wasn't stalking Dylan, but if the teacher had noticed, then Dylan must have, too. Students drifted into the room, glancing at her, wondering what she'd done. "Is that all?"

"Yes," he said and reached for a packet of passes. He spoke as he wrote, not noticing the many students who were sitting quietly at their desks, listening. Normally, there would have been chattering, but they didn't want to miss anything. "I've taught for almost thirty years. In that time, I've watched hundreds of girls throw themselves at young men at the cost of their education. Make sure you'ren't one of those." He ripped off the pass and handed it to her.

Refusing to make eye contact with anyone, she scooted out of the room and into the sanctuary of the hallway. Holding the pass prominently in her hand, she made her way to the English wing, hoping to lose her humiliation along the way. She doubted it would happen since there had been so many witnesses who would repeat the scene to infinity. See, she was learning something in math, but that was algebra, wasn't it? What would happen if she didn't go to English class? The thought tempted her. The stairs beckoned. At the end of the stairs, there was a set of double doors, her exit to freedom. All she'd to do was claim a dentist appointment when passing the campus security guard. It all sounded good in theory, except she hadn't have an office pass, someone to pick her up, or a car to drive away in. Might as well head to class. Escaping her embarrassing life would have to wait until latter.

Stella, her best friend, pantomimed wiping sweat from her brow as she entered the room. Leah dropped her pass on Mrs. Barkin's desk and headed to her place beside Stella. Her friend might have been concerned about her absence since they were working on a project together.

Leah managed to relate her personal disaster in hushed tones before their teacher descended upon them with a fluttering of hands. "Good, good, you're finally here. I wanted to address the two of you together."

The woman bent toward them, reinforcing Leah's bird imagery of her as she rested her long wings—make that, hands—against their table, giving the impression she sheltered them under her wings. In actuality, she blocked the other students from hearing her instructions. "Girls, I think you have a great topic about how people are shaped to be prejudiced by their religious views. Remember this is a persuasive speech. It isn't enough to say prejudice is rampant. Give personal examples. No one can dispute that. You also have to have more of a mission here. How is this prejudice ruining the world? Tell me how it can be changed. I want a call to action. Your essay in its present form is lacking that. Do you understand what I want?"

Leah and Stella nodded in unison as Mrs. Barkin smiled and headed on to a different group of students to help. Leah knew how to punch up the essay. Did she dare? It would mean risking possibly even more ridicule, even misdirected hatred. When she'd first started school, she'd been anxious. Her grandmother had bestowed a delicate silver pentacle on a chain upon her to keep her safe and strong and as a reminder of how special she was. Everything had been fine until another student had asked her about her necklace.

As she'd explained about the elements, a small group of students had gathered, interested in the necklace's powers. Unfortunately, she'd caught her teacher's interest, too. The woman had made a grab for the necklace, but had pulled her hand back suddenly, making Leah wonder if Nana had put a protection spell on it. The principal had insisted she could not wear the pentacle, claiming it disrupted the classroom. The necklace hadn't done anything. Leah had known that much at even a young age. First grade had been a hard year for her, but luckily, she'd already known how to read and write when she'd entered school, thanks to her father. It had been just as well because she'd often caught her teacher mouthing the words "devil child" whenever she'd been near.

Could she share this story? Would it make Stella think any different of her? The few times she'd been in Stella's house, no religious symbols had decorated the walls, indicating her mother wasn't overly religious. Failure to attend a church, mosque, or temple didn't stop people from claiming religious affiliation or the prejudices often attached to that religion. "What can we do different?"

Her friend held up one finger. "Well, I thought we might start with a quote from Buddha."

This was interesting. Her friend had never mentioned religion or Buddha before, but she'd also picked the topic for the paper. They could have gone with the easier ones about cloning, nuclear warfare, domestic abuse, or the dangers of GMOs.

"Which one?" She said the words as if she'd a head full of quotes by Buddha.

Gesturing to her pearl choker, Stella's expression became serene and distant, as if viewing an interior landscape only she could see. "We're all pearls on a string."

"That sounds good, but what does it mean?" Leah's experience with other religions consisted of televangelists, billboards, and people trying to shove tracts in her hand outside of movie theaters, warning her that movies were the devil's tools.

Stella blinked. "You don't know about Siddhartha's journey?" The surprise in her voice made Leah think she should have known. She might as well have announced she'd never heard of Abraham Lincoln or Santa Claus.

"You could tell me, but I thought we were talking about Buddha, pearls, and our essay." Leah could feel the tension leave her as her friend explained. "Siddhartha Buddha was his full name. Born a prince and married for love, he decided to see the people of his kingdom by walking through it. He discovered much heartache and poverty, which saddened him."

Stella finished waving one hand with a flourish. "That's why we're all like pearls on a string."

Leah didn't want to ask, but she did. "The man who had everything went for a walk and saw those with nothing. That makes us pearls how?"

Laughing, Stella touched her shoulder. "You almost have it. Buddha found all our actions have a profound impact on the universe. By having great wealth, lavish parties, and huge palaces, he took from people who barely had enough to feed their families. Of course, all the people in the kingdom have to give a tithe to the prince to enable him to do all this. In turn, he saw how everyone in the universe is connected. He, of course, changed his ways after learning this. Do you get it now?"

"Yes," Leah answered softly. She thought she got it. It made sense because she believed everything in the universe was connected. This was a side to Stella she'd not seen before. "If Buddha believed everyone was part of a giant pearl necklace, then those folks who believe some people are untouchables, others are going to hell, and still others just shouldn't be sharing the same air as them, they might regard everyone else as being loose pearls, not even on the necklace with them."

Her friend's fingers flew over the keyboard. "I'm getting this down. I believe we're going to have a great paper."

"What if no one understands what we're trying to say? They could be offended." Leah always worried about offending people, especially after the necklace incident. She understood on some level that just by existing on the same planet she offended some.

✧   ✧   ✧

STELLA SAVED THEIR paper and powered down the computer right before the buzzer sounded. Slipping the computer in its case, she grinned at Leah. "Why worry so much? It's not as if we're going to read it to the class. See ya later."

Her friend turned the opposite way as Leah headed toward the music wing. The hall grew less crowded since all music classes were electives. The higher-level ones required auditions, which was enough to discourage even musically inclined students. Even though Leah didn't like attention, she did like singing. When she sang, everything fell away. She didn't notice people around her. Truth be told, they were probably not paying attention to her, too busy gossiping, flirting, and furtively texting. Thinking about her solo, she didn't notice immediately all the other students were gone. The hall lights flickered and went out.

CHAPTER THREE

NO, NOT HERE, not now! She couldn't have a vision at school. She'd never had one during school. She could count the number of visions she'd had on one hand. Holding her hand high, she spread her fingers, noticing they appeared to be growing more transparent. Dropping her hand in horror, she looked down the hall, which went dark as the lights flickered out.

Great, was it a power shortage or what? Leah knew better as she tried to locate the skylights over her head. Nothing. The whole point of the skylights was to provide light. No light meant it wasn't daytime, or she wasn't in the school hallway anymore. A voice confirmed this.

"Make haste, Leah, before a long-nosed monk takes hold of you."

She recognized Henry, the unspoken leader from the night before. It didn't make sense that she was continuing her dream. Maybe even now she was drooling in her sleep in class, causing the other students to take photos of her with their camera phones without the teacher catching them. The thought caused her to shudder.

A forest formed around her with light filtering through the tree leaves. A few birds called from above her, and something rattled in the bushes near her. Her gaze traveled to her right where someone was coming toward her, possibly a teacher or a staff member to rescue her. Instead, an exasperated Sabina lunged toward her, grabbing her arm.

"No time for you to go simple. The witch catchers will fill you full of

needles, claiming they found the devil's mark when they themselves made the marks."

Leah stumbled alongside the woman who held her in a strong grip. Sabina was much stronger than she looked despite, being a few inches shorter and definitely a few pounds lighter than Leah. There was no way to resist Sabina's determination to save her from the witch catchers. Why would she want to resist?

Running beside each other, they reached the clearing where Henry and Margaret waited. The old woman in black wrung her hands, looking all the worse for their unexpected flight. Why shouldn't she? She'd lost everything to a villager's torch, burning her cottage and possibly her beloved pet. Henry's mouth firmed into a straight line as he spotted them. "I've a place we can use for the day to rest and decide what to do next. It is a small hut belonging to my cousin, which will give us refuge."

Moving onward, Leah gave silent thanks for Margaret who could not move as fast as the rest. Who knew people stuck in the middle ages were in such good shape? Leah guessed they had to be when running from people or animals who wanted to kill them.

They stopped only to take a deep drink at a stream. Leah watched all of them drop to their knees, scooping the water up to their lips with cupped hands. "Aren't you worried about…?" The word pollution stayed in her mouth. Instead, she knelt, carrying some of the cool water up to her mouth. It was delicious and refreshing. Dropping to her belly, she managed to get closer to the clear water, even immersing her face in it. Wonderful. A tug on the back of her head brought her face out of the water.

"No need for that. The witch catchers will surely drown you if they catch you." His voice rang with certainty.

Leah thought about protesting. She wasn't committing suicide, but decided against saying anything. Sometimes it was just better to follow orders. Back on her feet, she followed Henry's zigzagging trail. Occasionally he would run off the trail and circle a tree several times. When she caught her eyes on him, he explained with one word. "Dogs."

At last, they reached the small hut, little more than a thatched circular building with a hide-covered door and no windows. The four of them crowded into a space measuring no more than five feet at its widest point. The women reclined against the feeble walls while Henry stabbed his walking stick at the ground as if trying to uncover something. Eventually, he brought up a clay jar out of the ground.

The meager light streaming in from missing thatches and the imperfectly cut door illuminated the man and his find. The container released a vile smell. The other two women leaned forward eagerly as he shook out uneven off-whitish pieces that he passed out. Leah held hers in her hand, unsure of what to do with it, while the others crammed theirs in their mouths. It was food obviously, but what kind?

Her nose crinkled as it passed under her nose. Henry, noticing her actions, urged her to eat. "It is fish, girl. Might be all you get in a good long while. Do not waste time thinking about eating it. Just do the deed." The others nodded their heads in acknowledgment.

Leah placed the bit in her mouth and tried to bite through it with some difficulty. It looked and felt like the cuttlebone she used to put in her old parakeet's cage for him to rub his beak against. It tasted not like fish, exactly, but more like smoke, campfires, charcoal, or the liquid smoke flavoring Mother sometimes brushed on meat. They must cure the meat by smoking it. It made sense with salt being so expensive. She chewed meditatively as the other two put out their hands for more.

"Good fish," Sabina commented.

Henry agreed. "Yes, we're lucky Peter restocked the hut. Ever since his cousin from the next village died from her examination by the witch catchers, he's kept the hut stocked for whoever might need it."

Examination? Leah knew she didn't want to know, but she asked anyhow. "This examination happened when they were looking for the mark of the devil?"

"Yes," Henry answered, then placed a square of fish into his mouth.

"What is this mark of the devil when such a creature does not exist? He's a bogeyman made up by people who wanted to scare folks into accepted behavior." She related what she'd been taught, causing Henry to choke on his fish.

The man used his fist to pound on his chest. Henry stopped coughing but gasped for air a few times. He stood and announced, "I think I might go back to visit the water."

Sabina watched him go and then turned to look at Leah. "Talk like yours will get you branded a witch. No matter what you say, they would call you a witch, just to strip you naked and look upon your form before torturing you. I'm unsure if they hate all women or just the comely ones. It is certain that all those without a powerful family name or a man are certain to be accused."

"Are you saying these priests are pervs?" Leah knew the stories about the Burning Times, but none had suggested sexual perversion, or maybe she hadn't paid attention.

Sabina pursed her lips, trying out the word. "Pervs, I do not know this word. I know They're evil despite calling themselves men of God. That I do know. If they wanted to find the devil, then they would do well to hold a mirror up to their own faces."

Margaret seemed shocked at her words. "Be still, child. They might hear you. It will not go well for you."

Sabina sighed, her shoulders drooping. "It is not going well for me now."

Leah paused in the act of chewing and stared at her erstwhile rescuer, before asking, "What have you done that is so terrible?"

The dark-haired woman shrugged. "I'm a woman alone."

"Why should that matter?" Leah tried to remember what Nana had said, but she usually became so emotional when talking about the Burning Times, you'd think she'd lived through it herself. All her words ended up being indecipherable due to anger or garbled because of tears. Leah never understood half the things Nana said. The family knew never to bring up the topic, because it might cause another stroke.

Margaret answered instead. "An old woman alone has no merit or purpose in the village. With no children to call my own or to look out for me, it is easy to blame me when a cow refuses to give milk or a baby dies. If the village wants a culprit, my absence creates no loss."

Leah remembered being in the woman's home earlier, though she didn't remember when. Various spices and herbs had hung drying from the crossbeams. Margaret had secretly confided that she could even read, a skill usually limited to the clergy. As a young girl, she'd trained to be a nun, but when their motherhouse had broken up, she'd returned to her village. Some had whispered that God had rejected her. She'd used her knowledge to write down various recipes for possets and creams. No matter what the villagers whispered about her, they still came to her house for medicine. "They still ask you for help. I saw the woman at your door."

The old woman nodded in agreement. "That is true. When everything else fails, they seek my assistance." Margaret made some sign with her hand, causing Sabina to chuckle. "Ah, that's what I think of them. Some say I cause the illnesses as opposed to their over-imbibing or gluttonous natures. Those claiming I consort with the devil come to my door when the moon is full, begging for pennyroyal."

Pennyroyal. She remembered seeing a container of it in Nana's herb closet. She'd left it alone, although the name intrigued her. "What do they do with it?"

Both women looked at Leah in surprise.

The old woman rolled her eyes. "It can be used to chase fleas away. Those who asked for it did not overly care about fleas, considering the curs they chose to lay with." Both women giggled at the remark, which irritated Leah.

The language was difficult enough to make sense of without all the archaic metaphors. "Why would they sneak around at night to get some herb to get rid of fleas? Why not ask for it in the day?"

Waving a gnarled index finger, Margaret explained, "Their need was black, which is why they crept around at night. The pennyroyal would rid them of a child not of their husband's seed."

Sabina leaned in, motioning to the old woman with her hand. "For that they call her witch. I think they just want to get rid of her because she holds all their secrets."

"Makes sense," Leah agreed, wondering how Old Margaret managed to survive so long without someone offing her. "How old are you?"

The woman bit her withered bottom lip as her eyes flicked upward in the thin light. "I believe I've survived forty-four winters."

Forty-four! Her mother was the same age. She certainly didn't look anywhere as old as Margaret did. Nana didn't even look as old, and she was dragging her leg, too. Apparently, life had been harsh in the past. What year was she in? Better yet, what century? "Do you know what year this is?" Both women looked confused at her question. "What century is it?"

She thought she could at least pinpoint a general date. The women instead looked at each other as if they didn't understand her words or at least the meaning behind them. Even though she didn't understand every word she'd a feeling the language was supposed to be English.

"Am I in England?" Both women bobbed their heads and smiled.

Sabina pointed to Leah. "Do you be Welsh? I heard the people of Wales be dark."

Leah held out her arm, trying to see it as someone else would. She didn't see herself as dark, far from it, especially compared to some of the other students in her school. They might consider her dark, having no experience with people beyond their small village. "No, I'm American. I told you this *before."*

Margaret narrowed her eyes, displaying her doubt, while Sabina cocked her head. "You still be foreign and fair, which would be enough to condemn you as a witch."

The sound of footsteps nearby caused the three of them to freeze, casting anxious glances toward the door. The door opened slightly, allowing in enough sunlight to temporarily blind them.

"No fear, it is only I," Henry called out to the sunblind women.

Leah blinked a couple of times to bring her vision back to normal. The familiar outline of Henry began to take shape and solidified once he closed the door behind him.

"Have you ladies been gossiping about me?" he teased.

Shaking her thick hair back, Sabina sighed. "Our tongues recounted the evil of the witch takers and how Leah should take care, being foreign and fair."

Henry nodded, his weathered face taking on a solemn cast. "It is easy to blame the priests, even the church, even the King's soldiers, who allow the witch hunts to go on unabated, but the real evil lies in jealous, voracious hearts. Sabina's only crime is being prettier than all the other lasses in town. No fault of her own that her man died. Many village men cast lustful stares at her. Some less careful ones did so in the presence of their wives. Her beauty and friendliness earned her the witch label. All three of us are people who discommoded someone."

Leah stretched out her hand to touch Henry's shoulder to offer him some comfort, but her hands encountered a cool concrete brick wall instead of a rough woolen shirt. Flexing her fingers, she recognized the feel. It was how the walls in the hall felt. Henry's voice along with Sabina's grew distant as their bodies grew dimmer, like fading images on a movie screen.

Her environment became lighter, until she realized she was in the hallway, fingering the walls.

"There you're," a male voice chirped behind her. The sturdy figure of the school principal, Mr. Sharpe, strode up to her. When Leah had started school, she'd at first thought his rotund belly and handlebar mustache indicated he would be a jolly fellow. Appearances could be deceiving. The frowning man reached her.

"Ms. Carpenter, your choral teacher, reported you skipping. Where have you been?" Principal Sharpe faced her, leveling a belligerent look that dared her to utter some type of falsehood he could denounce to earn her another detention.

"I was here. Right here. I may have been late, but not that late, I think." Skipping didn't happen until you were more than ten minutes late, at least. Until then she was only tardy, which most teachers overlooked.

He folded his arms and sucked in his lips. If he thought that made him look more intimidating, Leah was more than willing to concur. "So, Carpenter, you mean to tell me you were here in this hall for the last ninety minutes? People passed through the hall on the way to lunch, but no one saw you? Is that what you mean?" His voice became louder as he growled the words.

No doubt, he'd never believe she'd just evaded witch hunters and had spent the last period in not-so-merry old England. Instead, she just nodded.

He grunted his disbelief. "Come with me."

That's what she'd been afraid of. Couldn't get a break in either century. In this one, she could expect to live a little longer, though.

✧   ✧   ✧

LEAH SAT IN the seat placed at an angle to the principal's desk. No one had to tell her it was where all previously nabbed students sat. The residual anxiety, fear, even defiance surrounded her as she adjusted her bottom on the vinyl-covered chair. The presence of so many negative emotions overwhelmed her senses, making her nauseated. A quick look up through her eyelashes showed Principal Sharpe peering at his computer screen, most likely looking up her home phone number. The obvious solution would have been to ask her, not that all students in trouble would furnish the appropriate answer. Then again, some might not even know their parents' number. They were used to having numbers programmed into their cell.

A pair of soft upholstered chairs beckoned to her. From their location in front of the desk and the fact they appeared comfortable, Leah guessed they were for parents and visiting school officials, not for skippers. If she asked to move, the answer would be no. Her excuse for moving could be she'd a psychological fear of puke green as she glanced down at the ugly greenish covering of her chair. Nope, that would just make her sound even weirder.

Residual emotions emanated from the chair, wrapping around her, echoing with the possibility of losing one foster home placement only to go to a crummier one. One boy had realized this was the "one more thing" his mother constantly threatened that would send him to live with his father and his new family. One girl had become so frightened the principal might find drugs on her that she'd wet herself. Yuk! That settled it. She quietly moved to the chair in front of the desk. Forget about asking, she refused to sit in that chair one second longer.

Principal Sharpe merely raised a questioning eyebrow, but continued to hold the phone up to his ear. He probably didn't want to yell into the phone when someone was picking up. Could be he thought she was already in enough trouble. What did one more thing matter? Leah considered the vacated chair with a baleful look. She'd never considered herself empathic with the ability to pick up unspoken emotional responses from others. Nana had concluded once, after watching a

Sherlock Holmes episode, that the detective must have a touch of psychometric ability to pick up objects and know so much about the person who used them. Leah had never pointed out his powers of observation solved the crime as opposed to some mystical ability.

THE PRINCIPAL RELATED her crime of missing chorus and apparently lunch. Her stomach growled, confirming the fact. Her hands gripped the soft padded arms of her current chair. A thought seeped into her head of the principal as a jackbooted thug who had never taught a day in his life. Great, now she was receiving parent impressions, but why would a parent know about his lack of teaching experience? Good chance she'd picked up a teacher's reflection. Some staff member called to the office, probably feeling just as victimized as she did.

Principal Sharpe hung up the phone. He stared at her, using what she knew he felt was his most intimidating stare with downturned lips and narrowed eyes. Great Goddess, what was happening to her? How did she know, without a doubt, this was what Sharpe considered his best glare that usually had the kids' knees knocking together, especially non-defiant students like her? The tall, broad-shouldered boys with attitude who enjoyed jaw jacking scared him. She blinked. Had she just read his mind? She was almost sure of it.

"Leah Carpenter," he started in a firm, deep voice. "Your grandmother is coming to pick you up. You're suspended for the rest of the day for your actions."

She bobbed her head in acknowledgment, unsure if a response was expected. Suspension for the day, was he kidding? Talk about stupid punishments. If she'd been the type of student who skipped class, a school suspension would have been a reward. Nana was coming to get her. Good, it would give them alone time to talk about all the weirdness suddenly constituting her life.

The scent of smoke clung to her. Turning her head a little, she managed to sniff her shoulder. Definitely smelled like smoke, not cigarette, but rather wood smoke. Which didn't make any sense unless her spontaneous trips to medieval England were more real than she'd previously imagined?

Principal Sharpe fiddled with a pen on his desk, and then pushed up suddenly. "I'll have my secretary notify you when your grandmother arrives." He disappeared out the door, leaving behind apprehension of Nana. He'd left because he'dn't wanted to talk to her grandmother. *The old crone gives me the creeps* had been his last thought, which would delight Nana.

Leah stood and walked around his office. If she were the type to snoop, now would be the time. Slowly circling the room, she drew closer to the computer screen displaying a screensaver of the school building. What had she expected? Babes in bikinis? Sharpe would be the type to have a camera in his office to film what the students did after he left.

Opening her senses, she searched for a camera hidden somewhere. No camera. How did she know there wasn't one? Hard to explain, but she'd a sense of certainty, perhaps similar to what Sherlock Holmes had experienced. Pulling out the corner of her polo, she wrapped her fingers in it and pushed the mouse. Her information popped up. Discipline record was clean except for a bold notation about skipping class with suspension being the consequence. Again, she shook her head at the idea of it being a punishment.

In theory, the teachers were supposed to deprive her of her makeup work so she'd receive a zero for the day. Students normally in trouble never asked to make up their work, so what did it matter? Good students would still ask for makeup work and get it, with a warning not to mention it to anyone. Stella had told her this after her own suspension resulting from enthusiastically welcoming a foreign-exchange student who had mistaken her friendliness for bullying.

A click took her to Teacher Concerns. A small note from Miss Santiago indicated concerns about the trio of girls bullying Leah. Well, she'd that right. Despite the note, there had been no follow-up. Geesh, she'd have received more attention if Principal Sharpe had thought she might turn into an international incident. Good students received suspensions, like herself and Stella, while bullies practically ran the school.

The rumble of a car engine drew her attention to the window in time to see Nana emerging from a cab. Stepping away from the computer, Leah headed to the door. Snatching up her book and purse, she made her way out to the secretary's desk before she called her. Outside in the outer office, she tucked in her shirt, hoping no one noticed her actions. All she needed was a uniform violation added to her formerly clean discipline record. The secretary gave her an apologetic smile. Well, at least one person didn't think she was guilty of the crime.

The tap of her cane announced Nana before she showed. Always one to look at the bright side, her grandmother had announced the stroke that had left one leg weaker than the other was just the excuse she needed to use her ornate silver wolf-head cane. It was an elaborate stick, which looked as if it might have served in a horror movie, which was probably why Nana liked it. While her father avoided attention, Nana treated it as her right.

Her grandmother came in with a smile and headed to the sign-out sheet. She signed Leah out with a jingle of her bracelets. Leah joined her grandmother, taking the arm that didn't wield the cane.

Her grandmother greeted her with a jovial air. "So what trumped-up crime have they tried to pin on you?" She said it loud enough so anyone could hear.

Wincing a little, Leah shrugged, not wanting to discuss it in a hallway filled with students. Bad enough they would see her leaving, but most would consider she'd an appointment or was sick. The others wouldn't even notice. Having only her geometry book, she wondered if she should get her other books. Leah abandoned the idea. She'd homework all right, but it had more to do with finding out why she suddenly sensed thoughts and took impromptu trips into the past.

Principal Sharpe was nowhere in sight. Probably a good thing. He would not have to explain in excruciating detail his version of the story. One of the good things about her family was they actually listened to her.

Their former neighbor had accused Leah of terrorizing her overweight basset hound. What Mrs. Higginbottoms, the neighbor, had been unwilling to admit was Theodora, Leah's cat, had chased and cornered the cantankerous canine. Apparently, the dog had had to have extra anxiety medicine that day. Leah had arrived on the scene when she'd heard the woman's cries and the angry snarl of her feline, along with some pitiful whimpering. Her family chose her version of the story over the outraged neighbor's dramatic account.

CHAPTER FOUR

N O SOONER HAD they scooted into the back seat and slammed the taxi door than her grandmother turned to her with a knowing look. "Come into your powers, have you?"

"Nana, please." She angled her head to the cab driver, hoping to convey her need for privacy. A snort answered her pleas as they both settled into the tobacco-smoke-tainted back seat. Wasn't there supposed to a smoking ban in public places? Then again, it might have been her. Turning her head, she sniffed the shoulder of her uniform shirt again. Still smelled like wood smoke, pine trees, and that disgusting fish she'd eaten. How could that be?

Her grandmother leaned over and sniffed her clothes, too. A thoughtful look crossed her face as she pointed to Leah's ankles, which were caked with mud and leaves. Where had that come from and why hadn't the principal noticed? Nana said nothing, honoring Leah's desire not to talk publicly.

The scenery outside the cab window included brown grass and withered leaves on the trees. The drought hadn't dealt well with the area. It took rain usually to make mud. She picked a small green leaf from her mud-encrusted legs. Twirling it between two fingers, she knew it hadn't come from here.

Where would she have encountered mud and green leaves in the few short steps from her father's sedan to the school doors? The flight through the woods had garnered the mud and leaves. It had been real, not a vision or daydream. If her run through the woods with Sabina, Henry, and Margaret had happened, then that meant the man in the throne-like chair existed. Remembering the man's crazed eyes and hate-filled voice caused her to shiver. How could she stop this?

The ride home in some ways was more like a funeral possession, slow and somber. If she couldn't think of a way to stop taking these return trips, it might end up being her funeral. Would her death in the past prevent her from being in the present? All she really knew was she didn't want to test out any theories. She looked at her grandmother for answers, and the woman took her hand and squeezed it.

"Be at peace, my little bird." Nana managed a smile that didn't quite reach her troubled eyes.

The driver coasted to a stop in front of their house. Leah opened the door and waited as Nana painstakingly counted out the fee, plus an appropriate tip. Once out of the cab, Leah turned slowly, peering at the familiar, run-down neighborhood. Most of the houses were older ranch-style homes showing their age with peeling paint, crooked shutters, and crumbling driveways. Most of them were rentals with property owners too penny-pinching to fix the places up. Why should they when a renter might just destroy their efforts? A house two blocks down sported a perfect green lawn and freshly painted shutters. An older couple owned it.

The rental houses served only as a stop on the renters' journey to somewhere else. Leah wished desperately for a house to call home, rather than a rental. She'd never had a tree house or marks on an interior doorframe to show how she'd grown over the years. Instead, her family worked hard not to change anything, from paint to landscaping, because it was not their home. The modest home boasted a basement where a few boards, drywall, and a door suggested the possibility of another bedroom. Her brother slept in the unfinished room with exposed wiring.

Even though it was petty of her, she was glad it was him, instead of her.

The neighborhood didn't show any signs of transforming itself into another time.

Nana snagged her arm as she moved her cane to her other hand. "Let's go and deal with your trouble."

Just like that, her grandmother had made it sound like she'd a report to write. She could imagine writing such a report. She could title it *How I Slipped through Time*. The subtitle could be *How I Was Almost Burned as a Witch*. Although, what she could remember about the Salem witch trials from a television special was some girls started it trying to cover their own attempts at divination. They wanted to see the faces of their future husbands. No one had ended up burned at the stake, just hanged, probably their version of being humane.

Nana unlocked the door and pushed it open. The smell of scorched coffee greeted them. Leah rushed to the kitchen to turn off the coffee-maker. Often, mornings were chaos as they all headed off their separate ways.

Following more slowly, her grandmother entered the kitchen. "Aye, the coffee. I guess that would be my fault, even though I never touch the stuff." Nana pulled out a chair and collapsed into it. "Could you make us some tea, sweet pea? I believe we're going to need it."

Grabbing the battered teapot, Leah filled it with water and set it on the stove to boil. Remembering she'd missed lunch, she also got out a small plate, arranged some almond cookies on it and placed it on the table. She picked out two mugs and bent to search for the tea bags. Her grandmother came up behind her silently, startling her when she spoke.

"Not those mugs. I need cups and saucers. I will get my special loose-leaf tea." Nana weaved a little bit as she held onto the counter for balance.

Leah didn't like tea, but usually choked down a cup to please her grandmother, who often treated it like a magical elixir. The loose tea was the worst, with the ground-up tea leaves getting in her mouth, often choking her. If she caught them before they slid down her throat, there was always the issue of spitting them out gracefully. So far, she'd managed to deposit them in a napkin while pretending to wipe her mouth. The loose tea was for fortune-telling.

The ritual was a familiar one. Not that Nana had used it to tell her fortune, but Leah had witnessed some of the regulars having their fortunes told. Some of the ladies liked it better than the Tarot cards, feeling it didn't compromise their religious beliefs. It was more like an elegant parlor trick, since they drank tea while doing it. Nana charged the same.

Her grandmother found the tin of tea and lurched to the table with the tin under one arm. Leah shook her head at her determined grandmother. Why hadn't she stayed seated? Leah could find the tea on her own. The sounds of objects falling alerted her Nana was on the move again. The sound of cursing led her to the living room, where several candles rolled across the wooden floor.

Leaning against the server that had previously housed the candles, her grandmother pointed to a white column candle half hidden by the couch. "I want that one, for protection. I need the purple one, too, to enhance my psychic senses and as an offering to Minona."

Leah preferred not to have the fuss of the whole lighting-candles-and-casting-a-circle thing. For a while, she waivered, not certain she even believed any of that stuff. All it had ever done for her was solidify her loner image. Different wasn't good, especially if she'd to keep re-inventing herself with each move. Her life would have been easier if the Sabbats and rituals fell on the traditional school holidays. Still, at this point, she should take all the charms, amulets, and protection she could get.

Kneeling, she gathered up the candles. Nana leaned against the server, favoring her bad leg and warned. "Don't get old, Leah. Even simple things become impossible tasks."

Leah looked up from her position and noticed her grandmother sported a half smile. "I'll do my best, but I think it's inevitable." She placed the column candle on the server as she bundled the others back into the box from where they'd fallen. "Is that all you need?"

Nana already had the purple candle in her hand. Pushing upright, she walked back to the kitchen. "Yes, it is enough. I'm only going to call on Minona today."

Leah followed her. "Not calling on the elements, then?"

Her grandmother turned suddenly, causing her to wobble a little. Her voice was firm but trembled with something. Leah couldn't decide if it was anger or horror. "I always call all the elements. You'd do good to remember that, young lady."

Of course, Leah knew that. The teapot whistled as they entered the kitchen. "Do you want me to handle the leaves and pour?" Normally, her grandmother fussed with the tea for her clients, making a huge ceremony out of it.

Nana centered the candle on the table, before answering. "It is better if you do it. I want as much of your energy on it as possible, since we're telling your fortune, not mine."

Pulling out a teaspoon, Leah measured the leaves for each cup, and then poured the steaming water into the delicate wide-mouthed teacups. "How come you always fix the tea for your customers?"

Her grandmother snorted as she cleared the table surface, arranging a cup of water, a stone, and an incense cone at various intervals. "I can't depend on any of them to do it right. Secondly, they would consider making tea something a servant does, which would be why I have to make it. In the end, it doesn't matter too much for my women since their lives seldom change overly much. They just come for reassurance that they will continue to lead their well-fed, easy lives. You, on the other hand, have much going on."

Leah had always wondered why the same middle-age women continued to come to Nana. They weren't single and looking for love, nor were they businesswomen hoping to start a new project. They were married women who had devoted themselves to a high-earning husband and raising spoiled children and pampered pets. They'd ask about vacation plans, remodeling the house, and plastic surgery, nothing too serious or earth-shattering. A few didn't even follow the advice Nana gave, much to their regret.

The image of one of the regulars, with her oversized lips resembling flotation devices, made Leah shudder. Nana had told her not to have the procedure done, but she hadn't listened. Now she'd to wait it out and hope her lips would return to normal over time.

Leah stirred in three teaspoons of sugar then carefully carried the thin saucers supporting the cups to the table, sloshing only a little bit. Probably would have been better to pour the tea at the table.

Nana reached for her cup, took a sip, and sighed. "Ah, just the way I like it."

Leah pulled out a chair to sit down when her grandmother pinned her with a look and an inquiring eyebrow lift. "Since you're up, why don't you cast the circle?"

It really wasn't a request, but rather an order. Leah started to walk around the table, but her grandmother stopped her. "Get the salt, the sea salt. This is serious. We don't want any bad energy or spirits messing with the reading. Come to think of it. It is fortunate you were sent home today so we could have a quiet reading without interference."

Fortunate might not have been the word Leah would have used. It was serendipitous how everything had worked together.

Her fingers fisted around the salt in her hand as she tried to clear her mind of woods, baying dogs, and the skeletal man on the throne. Breathing deeply, she counted to twelve before walking clockwise around the table, spreading a thin line of salt behind her. Nana welcomed the elements as she walked. Turning to the east, she lifted her hands. "Welcome, Air, breath of life." She touched a lit match to the incense cone.

Leah pivoted and raised her hands in a southern direction. "Welcome, Fire, symbol of warmth and passion."

Nana placed her fingers in the cup of water, pulling them upward, allowing the water to trickle off her fingers. "Welcome, Water. Mother, life giver, and nurturer."

A crystal embedded in the stone reflected the flickering light of the candle. Nana placed her hand over the stone. "Earth, Mother Earth, from which all life springs, welcome."

Leah finished walking the circle and stood while Nana held a match to the white candle flame to light the purple candle. Holding up her hands in a beseeching manner, her grandmother took on a majestic and commanding tone. "Come, great Minona, Goddess of Fortune-Telling, and help us now. As you helped the people of Togo predict the future with palm kernels and cones, help me now read these humble tea leaves. Great praise and gratitude are offered up to you, wise Goddess." Her grandmother sat down.

At least that answered the question of who Minona was. Leah had had her cards read dozens of times but never tea leaves. "What do we do now?"

Her grandmother gestured to her cup. "You drink your tea, but make sure to leave a little liquid so the leaves can flow free to form shapes. We also talk. Cup your hands around the bowl of your cup to give it energy. Tell me, child, all that is happening to you. I've felt a disturbance."

Leah took a sip of cooling tea, wondering where to start. "I've been having these visions that feel real. Look at my legs." She stretched out a leg to show her muddy ankles. Nana reached out a finger to wipe up some mud to hold it up to her face. She rubbed her fingers together, feeling the mud texture.

"This is not from around here." She held the mud up to her nose and sniffed it. "Lots of humus in it, rich soil, probably from a forest with decaying matter. Tell me how your legs got so muddy."

The story of running from the witch catchers tumbled out. Her grandmother didn't look surprised, only interested. Occasionally, she'd hold up a finger as if counting only to put it down, encouraging her to continue speaking with a gesture. Finally, Leah stuttered to a stop, aware of the fantastic nature of her tale now that she'd actually said it aloud.

Nana looked thoughtful as she rubbed two fingers against her brow where the third eye resided. "What is your name in these visions?"

"It is Leah, the same as it is now." An odd question. What could the meaning be behind it?

"Do you remember the clothes you wore?"

Good question. Had she spent much time looking down at herself? "The first time I wore rough, homespun garments. I saw myself as in third person. I didn't realize the woman was me until she pushed the hair out of her face. The second time I had on similar garments, but I tried to explain I was from America, but they didn't seem to understand. The third time, I don't remember, but I'm dirty from running through the forest."

"This is odd," Nana said. That was the understatement of the year. "Drink your tea." Leah picked up the cup, sipping and listening. "Many things are going on. It is possible you're returning to a previous life. If so, why are you physically returning? This is something I have never heard of before. If an earlier you held your spirit and existed in the past, why would the twenty-first-century you need to be present, too?"

Another her? Leah loosely believed a person could have several lives, but she'd never bothered to explore any of her past lives. What might this other her be like? She might have a boyfriend or was already married. People married much younger then.

Pointing to her teacup, Nana asked, "Done yet?"

A small residue of tea remained over the leaves. She nodded, waiting for instructions, hoping something useful to keep her safe and guide her while putting an end to her impromptu trips could come out of this reading. Cerberus, her three-headed mean-girl monster, was preferable to the evil man on the throne chair.

Nana held up one finger. "Follow my instructions exactly. Swirl the remaining liquid three times in your cup, then turn it over in your saucer, take three breaths, then lift your cup."

Holding the china cup in her hands, Leah gently swirled the liquid. She placed the cup on the table, placed the saucer on top of it, and inverted it. Taking three shallow breaths, she carefully lifted the cup. Brown liquid oozed across the saucer, leaving stranded piles of tea leaves scattered across the surface. It didn't look like an answer. It didn't look like anything.

Her grandmother must have sensed it and covered her right hand with her own. "Be at peace, child. Let me see what the leaves have to say. Hmmm."

Leah leaned closer.

With one finger, Nana pointed to lines almost making a loop. "Broken loop means disruption and trouble in your life."

"I got that already." Her top teeth sank into bottom lip as she tried to find symbols in the leaves. A streak with a rounded head caught her eye. "What about that? It looks like a comet. What does it mean?"

"Good eye, Leah. It is a comet, which signals change, even a pivotal event." Nana cocked her head, first one way and then another, searching for symbols.

"Will the change be good or bad?" She feared she knew the answer, but crossed her fingers underneath the table anyway.

"Ah, I see a wolf, a rose, and a hand." Nana looked up. "Change is change. It just is. A man who loses his job thinks the change is bad until he gets a better job, then the change is good." Her bracelet jingled as she waved her hand for emphasis.

Leaving school early was a change that had worked in her favor. "What do those other symbols mean?"

Her grandmother fixed her with one of her enigmatic stares, probably the same look that had had Principal Sharpe running to hide. "A rose means new love."

A smile appeared as she thought of Dylan. It could happen and was certainly not as weird as appearing in a different century. "The hand, what does it mean?"

Nana held her hand open, demonstrating what she saw in the saucer. "That is destiny. Karma. Right now, what is happening to you has a higher purpose you might not understand immediately, but you will." Balling up her fist, she flourished it. "What do you think this means?"

"A fight." She answered without thinking. Even in this, her grandmother was teaching.

"You're correct, or an argument." She pointed to a small symbol that resembled a tiny dog. "The wolf symbol troubles me."

"Are you sure it isn't a tiny dog? A Chihuahua might chase me. Maybe Ethan will finally get the puppy he's wanted," Leah joked, trying to elevate Nana's somber mood.

"No, it's a wolf. This I know. Did I not call on the great Minona to assist me in the reading?" She looked at the white candle.

Leah stared at it, too, waiting for the Goddess to appear in the flame. Fortune-telling used to be a pleasurable activity. Her grandmother was always one to give happy news, believing you would find out the bad things on your own. She'd also pointed out that bad news didn't earn any tips or follow-up visits. A happy customer left on the lookout for good fortune and recognized it when it came. "The wolf?"

"Someone close to you will betray you," Nana said, slowly raising her face to meet her eyes.

"In this century or the other?" She could probably survive a modern betrayal, but she wasn't sure about one in the past.

Leaning over the saucer, Nana traced an outline in the air. "I cannot tell you when these things will happen. My clients only exist in one century, but I think I see a bag in this last pile of leaves."

"A bag? As in paper sack?" Leah wasn't too sure she wanted to know what it meant, but a warning could help. She couldn't fight the enemy if she didn't know what to expect.

Turning the saucer gently, Nana moved the elusive bag closer to her. "I'm unsure if it isopen. Age dims your focus."

"What difference does it make if a bag is open or not?" The reading experience was not as fun and upbeat as she'd hoped it would be. An eerie sense of foreboding similar to a wet blanket settled around her shoulders, chilling her and pushing her down with its soaked heaviness.

"It troubles me that I cannot see it clearly. A bag if opened is a form of escape, which means you can escape these odd trips to the Burning Times."

Escape, that was good, which meant no more return trips to the land of scary. Truthfully, the forest was nice and unpolluted, but she'd no desire to stay there. "What does it mean if the bag is closed?"

Sucking her lips in, Nana hesitated, and then said, "A trap."

A trap? Not exactly what she'd wanted to hear, especially paired with someone betraying her. But there was love, new love. In the end, it wouldn't matter if she'd love if she was stuck, or even died, in the wrong century.

"Nana, is that all it says? It's not exactly clear." Leah had expected more since her grandmother's reputation rested on her ability to make detailed and accurate predictions. Part of it was she kept the readings positive, too.

Placing her hand over Leah's, Nana squeezed it lightly. "Tea leaf reading is open to interpretation. Where I see a wolf, someone else might see a Pomeranian."

Her initial impression of gloom and disaster could be wrong, Leah grabbed a cookie, munched thoughtfully and swallowed before giving voice to her thoughts. "You could be wrong, then."

Nana's head came up like a dog scenting a rabbit, her dark eyes narrowed, as she said, "I'm never wrong." With such an expression, it was easy to see why Principal Sharpe had hidden. Even knowing Nana worked hard to create the image of a scary gypsy woman from the horror movies didn't make it any less effective. Her grandmother blinked, as if suddenly remembering to whom she was talking, and managed a weak smile. "What I meant to say, dear one, is we shape our destiny. These are symbols, road signs, to tell you what is out there and to beware."

That didn't make her feel any better. "Does it tell me what century I need to be looking for love and betrayal?" So far, she hadn't met any potential love interests running through the medieval forest. Henry was too old, although kind. Since people in the past aged rough, could be Henry was only twenty-two. She snorted at the idea. Besides, he did nothing for her.

As far as betrayal, she'd go for the mean-girl trio every time. That's how they normally acted, so how could it be a betrayal? She wasn't exactly friends with them. It wasn't a betrayal unless you trusted someone. That narrowed down the field big time.

Leah had learned early on not to trust people, not early enough, though. Whom did she trust? Her family, of course. They might irritate her, but they'd never betray her. There was Stella and Dylan. She trusted both of them. Dylan didn't know enough about her to betray anything, and Stella had her own secrets.

If not this century, maybe the dream century? All she knew were the three fellow runners. Old Margaret would probably turn her over in a heartbeat since she blamed her for the loss of her cat and home. Henry had too much character to turn her over. A man who stood up to the mayor and helped them to escape was not the type to stab her in the back. Then there was Sabina. The woman was near her age and friendly. If the twenty-first century had taught her anything, it was to be careful of people who pretend to be your friends. They too often weren't.

Opportunistic friendships, her father called them. People who be-friended you because they thought it might somehow benefit them, from getting on the dance team to hanging out with a particular guy friend. Perhaps they believed your momentary popularity would rub off on them. She'd gathered a small group of followers after her spirited defense of Jeremy, but most had fallen away after she'd failed to do anything else as interesting. The few who had hung on puzzled her. They were people who wanted to know her for something she'd done as opposed to who she was.

Leah needed to know more. Nana could use the Tarot cards, which had to be clearer than the leaves. "Could you…" she started to ask, only to hear the front door slam.

CHAPTER FIVE

ETHAN WAS ALREADY home. The clock revealed two hours had passed since her taxi ride. Her brother stumbled into the kitchen, holding his hand to his nose and sporting a darkening, bruised eye. Nana stood. Remembering the circle, she cut a doorway in it, reminding Leah to open the circle properly as she rushed to her grandson.

"What happened?" Nana's loud voice filled the kitchen, causing Ethan to cringe a little.

He reached for a paper towel to hold up to his bleeding nose. "Fight," he mumbled.

Opening the freezer door, Nana pulled out a bag of peas and handed it to Ethan. "Put that on your eye. I can tell you were in a fight. Why?"

Leah guided her brother to a kitchen chair. "Might as well tell all or Nana will take to the neighborhood to investigate. You know you don't want that."

Ethan grumbled something indistinct through his bag of peas and paper towel.

"What? I don't understand?"

Her brother might have been a pain, but he was her pain, and no one should have been slapping him around. Anger bubbled to the surface, making her want to run out the door and find the big bully who had hurt her brother. Probably the hulking kid down the street whose parents had held him back a grade to bulk up for sports.

"Monica." He whispered the name.

Doubting she'd heard right, Leah repeated the name. "Monica? The British girl who moved in after us?"

"Yes," her brother answered, refusing to look up.

"She's a girl," Nana added, stating the obvious.

"A big, angry girl," Ethan added, his cut lip garbling his words a bit.

Yep, she was big, and she did have an attitude. Leah agreed with her brother. It surprised her since she'd thought British folks were happy and polite. Turned out, she'd gotten that wrong too. "Why did she hit you?"

ETHAN SHRUGGED. "EMILY had a book about fairies. It was surprisingly real, as opposed to all the made-up cartoon nonsense. Monica sat behind us making jokes about fairies not being real. I may have told her to shut up. Emily might have, too."

"That set her off?" It seemed like a relatively harmless exchange children and adults often had, without any noses bloodied in the process.

"I dunno. We were getting off the bus, and she pushes into me and calls me a 'ginger beer.' I think she's playing with me, like calling me a Coke or something. I say, 'Same to you,' then she starts swinging."

Nana piped in, "I don't know why she'd call you a ginger beer. Isn't that like a root beer?"

Clearing her throat, Leah got everyone's attention. "I guess it is, in a way. Apparently, it's also a British slur for gay."

Ethan lowered the bag of peas. "She thinks I'm gay, and then I said she was gay?" His eyes flicked up, as if he was thinking. "She is a big girl with a bad haircut that makes her look like a boy from the 1950s. I bet I'm not the first person to call her gay."

Leah didn't correct her brother for going right to the stereotypes. "Then you understand why it might upset her."

"Yeah," he agreed. "Still, it makes no sense why she'd call me gay."

Leah was starting to wonder about her little brother, who had better fashion awareness than she did. Now, she was heading right into the stereotypes. There had to be a better way to make sense of it for her little brother.

Resting one arm on the table, she angled her chair in Ethan's direction. "Remember when we moved and how you had trouble fitting in?"

Ethan managed to bob his head in agreement while the bag of peas still covered half his face. "It was only a few months ago. Yeah, fifth grade is even worse with the gender polarization."

Nana cocked her head like a curious bird. "What?"

Leah tried to explain. "He means the girls only hang out with girls and guys with guys."

Her grandmother pulled the bag holding her deck of Tarot cards from her pocket and muttered, "That's the way it is supposed to be. You're ten years old."

She'd had the Tarot cards all along. It was peculiar she'd chosen to read tea leaves for her. Had she not wanted to see things too clearly or had she been afraid of what she might find? Despite her belligerent nature, Nana wanted people to be happy. The best way to do that was to tell them only the happy things.

Ethan grumbled about the injustice of his place in life, not limited by a swollen lip and a pea bag. At least his nose had stopped bleeding. It was almost impossible to make out his words with the tissue wadded up in his nostril. "Sports. That's all the boys ever talk about. Sports they watch on television, sports they're going to try out for, games they might attend, and sports players' stats. Yawn. I could understand if Monica had to listen to that. Still, she has girls to talk to who talk about everything." Her brother threw out his free arm for emphasis.

Leah was tempted to add that in her experience females didn't talk about much besides boys, other girls, and boys. Stella was an exception, which was one of the reasons she liked her.

Nana shoved the deck in front of Ethan, who automatically cut it, a little sloppy with one hand, but he still managed to stack one-half on top of the other. "Are you thinking of your question?"

For him, she pulls out the cards, Leah complained to herself. What was the difference?

Instead of turning the card over, Nana kept her cupped hands over the deck and asked another question. "Does Monica talk much to the girls in her class?"

Ethan fingered his lip, possibly checking the swelling, before answering. "I don't know since we'ren't in the same class. I see her outside in the hall or in the lunchroom. When I see her there, she looks just as angry as she did before she punched me. The girls avoid her. Don't blame them. If I hadn't stood so close, I wouldn't be freezing my face with frozen vegetables."

Leah teased her brother, who was starting to sound more like himself. "I imagine those peas are cooked now, considering all the hot air you've been putting out."

Ethan forced out a laugh at the same time Nana turned over a card.

The three of them stared at the Tower card. The old deck was familiar, as was the slightly leaning tower of stones that looked to Leah like it might tumble down at any time. Not exactly a strong symbol.

Ethan touched the card with an index finger and softly mouthed the word, "Turmoil." He looked up. "I know it indicates, but what does it really mean?"

"It depends on the question." Nana flashed a slight smile. "It could mean change is coming to your finances, spiritual plane, love life, or even health."

Lowering the pea bag, he gestured to his darkened eye. "I've already experienced the health change. What else can I expect?"

"This might not be a good time for financial investments. You may have a few revelations or insights. Things are not always as they seem. Those you may depend on to be there for you might not."

Ethan sat with a dumbstruck look on his face, staring off in the distance.

Seeing his expression, Nana hurried to offer, "I can turn another card for confirmation."

Waving his hand, Ethan protested, "Don't bother. I'm not sure I can deal with any more happy revelations." He pushed out his chair and left the kitchen without saying another word.

Leah watched her brother go, troubled at the absence of his usual happy demeanor. Growing up had a tendency to knock your feet out from under you. Her grandmother picked up the card and placed it back in the deck, reminding Leah of her frustration with the ambiguous tea leaf symbols.

"Nana?" She gestured in the direction of the deck. "Why no cards for me? You pulled out the deck as soon as Ethan had an issue."

The deck disappeared into a silk bag and returned to the skirt pocket. "Ethan is a child who needs clearer answers, while you're a woman who needs to find her own answers and make her own destiny."

You're a woman. Need to make your own destiny. Just yesterday, her father had informed her she couldn't take the car to drive to Stella's, despite having her driver's license, because she was too young. "The other day I was too young, now I'm to pick out my own destiny. How's that work?" Her voice grew louder with her frustration. Realizing she was yelling at her grandmother, she tacked on a "Sorry."

Nana reached forward to cradle a hand around Leah's chin. "My child, I wish it were easier for you, but it isn't. Destiny picked you, but you can shape your path somewhat. Something in your past life calls to you, unfinished business your soul must complete."

"What?" Leah shook her head as if trying to remove Nana's words. "How can I have unfinished business in the past? I've never heard of anyone returning to the past to tidy up things. This makes no sense."

Her grandmother's face drooped with sadness. "I wish I could take this trial away from you, but it is yours. It will be the making of you, even though you're already a strong person."

Trial? That never sounded good. She'd an image of the dark-headed young woman, who she knew was herself, being dragged into a court-room where a skeletal man in dark robes presided as judge and jury. There had to be a way to stop her unplanned trips. "If people travel back and forth through time, why can't they remember it?"

Her grandmother gave her chin a squeeze. "Good question. It shows you're always thinking. There are many reasons why people do not *clearly* remember." She emphasized the one telling word. "Often, they solved the problem in the previous life, so there's no reason to remember. They solved their karmic dilemma. Other times, only sections appear to us in dreams or a sense of déjà vu. Perhaps we see a stranger on the street whose spirit resonates with ours. It is someone from our previous lives in a different body. Our mind doesn't recognize them, but our spirit does."

"Is there a reason we don't remember everything? Life would be easier if you could use past-life knowledge. How can you solve a problem if you don't know what it is?" This time-traveling business was not only frightening her but also making her angry. Why couldn't her old self tell her new self what to do? Of course, her old self didn't seem to be lingering around to be of any use.

Nana stood and carried her used cup and saucer to the sink swaying slightly without the help of her cane. She strained off the tea leaves into one saucer to use in the compost pile. Papa teased her sometimes, calling it magickal compost, which yielded astounding vegetables and blooms. Looking out the window, she spoke. "I often wondered if it was like victims of violent crime whose brains bury the memories since living with the knowledge is too much. Then again, I heard a reincarnation expert speak on karmic destiny at the Spiritual Fair last year. You remember the fair?"

The fair was one of the few times she'd felt normal. Children dressed as elves and fairies had dashed through the various stalls that had sold everything from healing crystals to every type of incense a person could envision. The sheer volume of books addressing everything from reading auras to astral travel had staggered her imagination. A feeling of peace swept over her with the memory. "Yes, I remember it."

Nana continued as if she hadn't heard the wistful quality to her answer, or she'd chosen not to acknowledge it, saving her some embarrassment. "He said most people who try to recall previous lives remember only the moment of death clearly. If it is a violent death, the emotional impact is especially strong. It is also the closest memory to the new person."

"That makes sense," Leah replied, picking up the plate of remaining cookies. Her other self in the other time had definitely had a violent ending. She didn't even have to wonder about it. Would her current self prevent it or had it already happened? "Still, knowing what needs to be done would make things much simpler."

Her grandmother half-filled the sink with water, squirted in some soap liquid and whipped it into lather with her hands. "It should all be that easy. You'ren't born knowing what you did wrong in the previous life and knowing what you should do with this one. With each life, we encounter other people on their karmic paths, often souls we knew before. Together we have to discover our destiny and learn what we need to know."

Sealing the cookies into a plastic container, Leah asked aloud, "What if you don't do the thing you're supposed to do in your lifetime?"

Grandmother's voice, muted by the running water, still rang clear. "You have to repeat it in each new life until you get it right."

She'd thought as much without Nana confirming it. Her lips twisted to one side. No one needed to tell her this was not her first time reliving this scenario. Apparently, she hadn't gotten it right in previous lifetimes.

Her life depended on her making it this time. If she didn't die violently in the past, would it change her current life? Would she cease to exist? She'd a feeling if she died in the past, she'd die in the now, too. Would her family simply have one less daughter and never even blink when they heard the name Leah? This time she'd to succeed, and to do that, she needed knowledge. This called for a research trip to the library.

A need to have more information for the essay was how she framed her plans to both her father and Stella. He even let her have the car, which was strange since the other day she'd been too young. Had Nana said something? She'd chosen not to trouble her parents with her recent adventures. Not much they could have done. Her mother's mental health already bore too much stress from the recent death of two of her homecare clients. As a health care professional, she tended to take it hard when her patients died.

Her father would have given her a doubtful look if she confessed all. If they had been Jewish, he would have converted to Judaism. It was as simple as that. Or was it that simple? She used to bemoan her Wiccan roots, considering them an insurmountable obstacle to any type of future relationship with Dylan. Maybe they weren't.

No one her age had any use for religion, or anything vaguely similar to mainstream kind. There were a few born-again kids at school who wore enough cross jewelry to prevent them from ever getting through an airport metal detector. She chose not to enlighten them. Their symbol had come from an Egyptian sun-god culture a mere six hundred years ago. Even if she'd, they wouldn't have believed her. They were so thoroughly entrenched in their Bible studies, contemporary gospel music, and Christian fiction that they refused to examine the very world around them. They took every word their minister said as gospel. Yep, they were the only ones who never had doubts or questions.

Some folks might have called it great faith. On the other hand, it might just have been laziness, the fear of examining life, and all it entails, on their own. She'd even heard once, from one of her Christian friends, that to question anything could result in eternal damnation. That would certainly put an end to any thinking outside the religious box. What would they do if they were to found themselves caught in the same situation?

Would they think they were possessed? Would they call for the priest or run out in front of an oncoming semi? Hard to know, but in the end this was a fight resting squarely on her shoulders. She might not like it, but that didn't change the circumstances. This sudden knowing people's thoughts would help.

Taking the keys offered by her father, she tried to probe his mind. Nothing. Had her ability gone away as soon as it had occurred? Great, what now? She'd found a magic tool, but lost it a second later?

CHAPTER SIX

Leah drove to Stella's house, making sure to use her turn signal and come to full stops. Did her father know how to shield his thoughts? In a house full of Pagans, it might have been an important skill to have. She should try to read Stella. Walking through other people's thoughts was wrong, but how could she find out? She could pick a stranger as opposed to losing a friend.

Stella waited on her front step, clutching a notebook. Leah had barely stopped the sedan before her friend vaulted in, slamming the passenger door. Turning red eyes and a tight face her way, Stella said, "Let's get out of here now. I'm not sure if I can put up with those people a minute longer."

Leah reversed slowly out of the driveway. The thought of burning rubber to leave as fast as her friend had suggested crossed her mind only briefly. Such action would have resulted in the cancellation of any future use of the family car. "Those people" had to be Stella's parents, since no one else resided in their house. Besides, most teens battled with the limitations or demanding expectations of their parents, and a few were unlucky enough to have parents who wanted to relive the life they wished they'd had as a teen through their children.

A rock ballad played softly as raindrops pelted the windshield. Rain, just what she didn't need. Oh, well, she'd have to drive in all kinds of weather. She might as well get used to it. Stella sniffled occasionally, probably wondering why her friend wasn't asking her what was wrong.

Driving was difficult enough with trying to remember all the rules plus directions to the library. Why had she never paid attention when other people were driving? Then again, the issue of popping out of the current century into another was a bit disconcerting.

Her hands tightened on the steering wheel as she realized she could disappear in a flash, leaving the car driverless and her friend in danger. It would be hard to explain to her father when she returned. Make that if she returned. Stella sniffled again.

Leah sighed. "What happened?"

STELLA WIPED HER nose with the back of her hand. Leah reached for the ready supply of fast-food napkins kept in the car, handing one to her tearful friend.

"Boundaries, apparently my mother has none." She blew her nose, sounding almost like a honking cartoon character. Leah decided against mentioning it. Instead, she waited, knowing her friend would reveal all if given enough time.

Stella jerked at her shoulder belt impatiently as if it was the one guilty of offending her as opposed to her parent. "She snooped through my room. She calls it cleaning. Ever since my mother lost her job as an office manager, she has too much time on her hands. Obviously enough time to root through my room."

Leah would be upset if her mother rooted through her room, mainly because it would merit a lecture on being more organized. What could Stella have that would upset her mother? "So what did she find? Racy magazines, a suggestive love letter, some weed?" She laughed because she doubted her introverted friend would have any of the mentioned items, but you never knew.

Stella answered with an abrupt one-word reply. "No."

That was it. First, she blubbered until Leah asked, then she clammed up. Kinda hard to sympathize when she didn't know what to feel bad about. She braked for a four-way stop, paying attention to who arrived first to decide when her turn came. Luckily, only one other car was at the stop. He shot through the four-way, not allowing her to question who had the right of way. She'd have let him go first, but the sports car driver wasn't taking chances.

Information signs denoting a library nearby caught her eye at the same time Stella decided to enlighten her. "Hey, Leah, I'm sorry. I didn't tell you because I didn't know how you'd react. Certainly not like my mother, but I want to tell you."

"Go ahead," she encouraged, spotting the library building a couple of blocks down the street. Her friend couldn't tell her anything that would be too surprising.

"Well," Stella started and then stopped. She looked out the window. "I suggested the topic about religious intolerance and prejudice."

Leah flicked on the turn signal and pulled into the library parking lot. "It's a good topic. I've no complaints. In fact, I want to do a little more research on it today."

"Yeah, I know, but I never explained why I picked it." Stella turned a wary expression to her.

Twisting the key to turn the car off, Leah answered, "Okay." Stella's family had never struck her as overly religious. They might make it to church a half-dozen times a year, but she doubted anyone would be guilty of persecuting them. Her friend sat, inspecting her cuticles, probably waiting for her to say something else. "Why did you?"

"I've developed an interest in earlier religions, even Pagan ones. I've been studying them. New religions replaced them sometimes under the penalty of death. Convert or lose your head." She made a slashing motion across her neck. "Were you aware of this?" Stella's raised eyebrows expressed her outrage.

The thought of Nana's lectures on the subject crossed her mind. "I may have heard of it."

Stella visibly inhaled, as if steeling herself for something. "The more I read the more curious I became. Eventually, I started reading Wiccan books. That's what my mother found in my room. It caused her to go berserk, accusing me of being a witch and putting the evil eye on people. Are you shocked? Do you still want to be my friend?"

A genuine smile broke across Leah's face, and she surged forward to hug her friend only to have the shoulder safety belt cut into her neck and shoulder. Releasing the belt, she managed to wrap Stella in a tight embrace. "No worries, friend. I'm not shocked. You won't believe how not shocked I'm."

"Really?" The word tangled in Leah's hair as her friend returned the hug with vigor. "Why is that? Most people might be weirded out or something."

Leah laughed. "You met Nana."

"Right," Stella agreed, then chuckled. "You're the only person I know who has a grandmother who tells fortunes. I guess that makes you open to anything."

"Not quite anything," Leah murmured, easing out of the embrace. They were in a public place. "Too much hugging and we'll be the next girl couple at Silverton High."

"Oh, you didn't know? We already are, thanks to our own mean girls and their campaign to keep you and Dylan apart. It isn't going too well, though, thanks to my romantic interaction with Jacob 'Thinks He's God's Gift to Women' Collins." Stella mimicked polishing her nails on her jacket.

"What? What's this to do with you and Jacob? I thought you guys only had two dates?"

"YOU'RE RIGHT. WE only had two dates. I thought he was okay on the first date, so I agreed to the second. We kissed, but it wasn't anything special, no chemistry. Still, Jacob couldn't believe any lesbo wouldn't switch teams after dating him or at least that's what he'd want everyone to think. He made sure to tell everyone I was hot for him, as opposed to you. He may even give me another chance." Stella pretended to fan herself as if overcome by the thought.

"Lucky you," Leah teased.

Her friend agreed with a chuckle. "What I want to know is which mean girl has her eye on Dylan that Team Evil is willing to put so much work into painting you and me with the rainbow paintbrush."

What Stella suggested was something Leah hadn't considered. Brianna and Alexis had boyfriends, but that didn't stop them from flirting with every attractive male within range. Lauren, she didn't know. It might explain why they'd singled her out, then another thought occurred to her. "I guess I always thought it was me they picked on, but I think it's you. Could be that Lauren has her eye on Jacob."

Resting her hand on the door, Stella grinned as she swung the door open. "Well, she's welcome to him. I'm not standing in her way."

Leah hopped out of the car, making sure to lock it. The last thing she needed was for some slackers to decide to take the family car for a joyride. She waited for her friend to round the car to finish their conversation. "It could be Jacob has no interest in her, but she thinks you're the problem." It was rather like her three newfound friends from the Burning Times who took the blame for sheep dying and crops not doing well.

"Yay me," Stella said. "The bad thing is I can't do anything about it. If I pretend to ignore Jacob for some strange reason, it will make me more desirable. No matter what I do, I'm doomed."

"I know the feeling." Leah hadn't really thought about what she was going to do when she next appeared in olden times. Apparently, she didn't get to take things with her to prove she was not a local. Just as well. Something as innocent as an MP3 player would have been an instrument of the devil.

They entered the library, silencing their voices to escape the head librarian's watchful eye. The somber head librarian appeared to have a special dislike of children in all forms, expecting or afraid they would bully her offspring, the books, with dirty fingers or bent pages.

Stella looked up the books they needed in the online catalog. Most of them were not on the shelf. They managed to find a few books on anti-Semitism, but that was it. It appeared they weren't the only people interested in the same topic. It would be helpful if some of the books came back soon. The list of titles in hand, Leah searched for the reference librarian.

Both girls approached the reference desk quietly. A young woman, probably fresh out of college with her library science degree, looked up. "Can I help you?"

"Yes." Leah placed the list on the counter. "My friend and I are working on a report for school, but we can't find any of these books."

The librarian looked at the list and mumbled a bit under her breath before looking up. "Can't help you. I'm surprised They're still in the online catalog. They were stolen a while ago."

They weren't spell books. "Why would someone steal them? They're only history books."

The librarian nodded her head. "That's true, but they may have presented a more honest and complete picture of the witch trials and persecution. Plenty of people around here don't want that. We'ren't even going to order replacements. They'll just be stolen again."

Stella grumbled beside her. "My mother."

Leah turned in surprise. "What?"

"People like my mother are stealing them. I'm not saying my mother stole your books. I doubt she even knew they were here. Someone who doesn't want any diversity in his or her world."

The librarian looked intrigued. "Yes, these monotheists think they run it."

Another one? It always surprised Leah when she stumbled across someone not part of the dominant religions. There were Pagans all around her, or at least people who didn't march with the leading faith. All the same, it wasn't helping her with her report or her more important personal research.

Leah turned away, and the librarian called out, "Wait."

She bent low behind the reference desk, rattled some papers, and reappeared clutching a typewritten page with various Internet site names on it. "Here, this might help. You can use the library computers."

Stella snatched the paper and read it with an avid expression. Leah murmured her thanks, eager to pull the paper from her friend's hands. How weird was it that the woman would have the paper with all sorts of sites printed on it? Could be she'd pulled the paper out of her purse as opposed to a library file while rattling under the desk. Leah reached for the paper her friend held, but Stella slapped her hands away.

"I'm not finished." She hurried to a computer, leaving Leah to follow.

Her friend typed in the words to a site called Teen Witch. Looking over Stella's shoulder, Leah asked, "Do you think you'll get an unbiased opinion from such a site?" She knew the site and felt it was fair, but she wanted to know her friend's opinion before she revealed any of her own secrets.

Stella spun on the desk chair and regarded Leah with a mixture of scorn and surprise. "Seriously? You're asking me if I think the site is unbiased? I'm willing to bet it is more unbiased than any of those Holy

Roller sites. Everyone has an agenda or an angle to promote. I think it is to our benefit to check out all angles."

Leah agreed and scanned the paper for any site that might be beneficial to her, finding a registry of people killed as witches. She slid into a chair next to her friend and typed in the site address. What would she find? What did she want to find?

The site came up with a somber banner featuring old-time people standing on a scaffold, waiting to be hanged. Even though it was only a sketch, each person's face mirrored identical confusion. How had they ended up there?

Leah began to read. *This is an incomplete registry of people who were tortured and put to death due to the evil that often exists in the heart of men combined with the mob mentality, which results in the worst behavior of humankind. Make no mistake. Every bit as horrific as the Holocaust perpetuated on the Jewish race by Hitler. Unfortunately, not every name was recorded, due to the sudden violence of the acts. Often, people killed for being in the wrong place at the wrong time didn't even have a chance to give their names. Other times, no one cared. The surviving relatives worked to piece together a registry of sorts to remember those whose lives ended too soon.*

The search box beckoned to her. She first typed in Old Margaret's name only to find plenty who had died as accused witches. No help there. She typed in Sabina's name and got fewer names than with Margaret, but still considerable. Too bad, she didn't know anyone's last name. Still, Henry might work because not too many men had been witches. About two dozen popped up, obviously more than she'd thought. Looking around carefully, she noticed Stella was intent on writing something down that she'd found on her site.

She let her finger hover over the keyboard, unsure if she truly wanted to know. Then again, she might come up with nothing since the records did not have every name. She typed in Leah Carpenter, then pushed the enter key. An entry came up immediately.

Leah Carpenter, an unknown stranger to the town, sentenced as a witch to be burned at the stake.

She gasped, and her head snapped back, attracting Stella's attention. "Leah, what is it?" Concern filled her face.

"Um, nothing." She stalled, swishing the mouse to close the window. Her friend might have been open to other religions, but her best friend traveling through different time periods and running from witch catchers would have been a little more to swallow. That she might have to rescue the past Leah if she wanted to exist now would have been even harder. Still, she could use some help, even if it was only moral support.

She maximized the screen and turned the monitor so Stella could see it.

Her eyes flickered over it. "How weird that someone long ago had the same name as you. Creepy, is not it?"

"You have no clue." Despair flavored her voice, making it tired and flat.

Stella's face grew troubled. "You don't mean…" She pointed at Leah and then the computer screen, the obvious question apparent in her eyes.

"Yes, I do think it's me, which is the reason I wanted to find out more to avoid dying in some medieval village at the hands of angry peasants." She attempted a sheepish smile, hoping it didn't resemble indigestion more.

Stella shook her head slowly as if trying to shake something off. "Is this like some ancestor you're trying to get in touch with?"

"I wish." Things would have been a lot simpler that way. "Nope. For some reason I seem to slip into another time unexpectedly. I'm sure you heard about me leaving school today."

"Who hasn't? Gives you a few bad-girl vibes just to keep things interesting. I was waiting for you to tell me where you went. Did you sneak off campus? Go hide in the second gym like most of the skippers?" Stella wiggled her eyebrows at the last question. They'd both previously discussed the stupidity of skipping school only to end up hiding underneath the bleachers of the rarely used old gym.

Leah inhaled. Here it went. It was one thing telling Nana, who believed in astral travel, but she wasn't a hundred percent sure this was what was happening to her. "I wasn't in school today because I was in some hut at the edge of a forest, eating dried fish with three other alleged witches." She watched Stella mull over the concept as her eyes flicked up to the ceiling as she chewed her bottom lip. At least, she didn't immediately call her crazy.

"Bet you didn't mention that to Principal Sharpe."

The interest in her friend's voice indicated she didn't totally disbelieve her. "Nope, I kept insisting I was in the hall. I was surprised how much time had passed. It didn't seem that long. Maybe time moves faster when you're running for your life."

Stella touched her foot to hers. "Hey, what can I do to help?"

"I'm not sure. Believing me helps. I'm trying to find out what I can about that time to protect myself. You could cover for me if I disappear in the future. I can be walking down the music hall and suddenly I'm in the forest." The ability to flash in and out of centuries baffled her. It would have helped if some warning bell would sound, preparing her for the shift, but it never did. How a person prepared for such a thing baffled her. The best she could do was accumulate knowledge.

Stella agreed with a head bob and a somber countenance. "What else? That seems like such a small thing to do. I would have done that without knowing where you were."

Chewing on her thumbnail, Leah wondered what her friend could do. Stella was as good a student as, or better than, she was. Her friend hovered between going into law and becoming an investigative reporter. If you wanted to get to the root of something, you asked Stella to look into it. "I'm trying to find out more about the time I shifted to, thinking I could find something to help me when I do. Henry mentioned something about everyone dying a witch's death in a couple of German villages, even the children and priests."

"Goodness, that's hard to believe. Who's Henry?" Stella turned backed to the computer and typed in "witch hunts in Germany."

"Henry is the man helping us to escape the mob who wants to string us up or light a fire under us. I'm not sure what the prevailing method is." Leah looked over her friend's shoulder at the various sites that popped up. She pointed to one. "Don't bother going there. That man is whacked. Supposed to be a college professor or something, and he doesn't even know that King James deliberately changed the verse 'Thou shall not suffer a poisoner to live,' and substituted 'witch' for 'poisoner.' The prof definitely has an agenda to sow more hate and prejudice."

Stella continued to scroll down the entries, squinting. She'd a hard time focusing on print and refused to put on her glasses in public. She complained they made her feel like a little old lady. Leah figured it had something to do with her glasses making her look smart. Everyone knew smart girls were on the bottom rung of the flirtation ladder, unless some guy wanted to copy your homework. Neither one of them was desperate enough to fall for that obvious trick. Okay, maybe once, but never again.

Stella still stared at the screen. "I think I found it."

Leah leaned forward to see, and everything went black.

✧   ✧   ✧

THE DARKNESS BECAME gray, but still dark, with a few spots of brightness where torches glowed against stone walls. The rough stone floor chilled her bare legs. Fingering her skirt, she realized it was a rough homespun material. Guess it was too much to come back as a princess in jewels and satin.

Something heavy weighed down her arms. A large hand wrapped around her slender biceps. Make that, one around each arm. An upward glance revealed a pair of muscular brutes. One cracked a grin, showing his rotted teeth. Apparently, dental care didn't rate in this time.

"Bring the prisoner closer," an authoritative voice rang out.

Leah was betting it was her skeletal friend, but she couldn't see him. Expecting to walk, she pushed up with her quads as the thugs pulled her upright. Stifling a moan, she experimentally put her weight on one foot. Her leg crumpled as if it was wet spaghetti. Instead of letting her fall, her guards held tight to her arms and dragged her the few yards.

A pair of lit, tapered candles revealed that once again she faced her good buddy, making her question why the two of them appeared bound together in some type of karmic dance.

"Closer." The guards dragged her a few steps closer. "Now, leave." He clapped his hands, treating the guards as no more than trained dogs.

The men dropped their hold. The sudden loss of support caused her knees to crash into the hard stone, making her wince in pain.

"Not so high-and-mighty now, are you, Arabella?" The man purred the words as if delighted. He put his bony fingers on his knees and leaned forward, attempting to look in her eyes.

Leah wiggled her toes and fingers. They all worked, but why had her legs refused to hold her? It made no sense. The man called her Arabella, which could be her name in this time. He said it as if he knew her, which made it personal. Who knew? Could Arabella have done something bad to him? It might explain why she wasn't already dead. She flexed a shoulder as she pushed up into a seated position. The motion hurt, but she could still manage, which was a plus. Still, there was this man. Truth might serve her for once. She hoped it would.

"Excuse me, sir. I think you mistake me for someone else. My name is Leah." She crossed her fingers, hidden under her skirt.

"Leah." He said the name and laughed. "Taking on the name of the less-favored sister will not save you. You were always Arabella, even though your parents chose to give you an elegant name much above your station. They hoped for something better for you than to be a wife of a farmer or a traveling tinker. Maybe you did as well."

His dark eyes stared into hers without blinking. She turned away, never any good at these staring contests. He wanted something from her, but what? A confession of some sort? It was personal. No doubt about it. Henry thought those accused of being witches had been on the wrong side in political battles. Margaret had declared it was because she'd no husband or family to stand for her. Sabina had blamed her accusation on being too pretty and single. It was enough to damn her in most of the town women's opinions.

She scooted her legs underneath her, ready to rise. Her muscles trembled, spasmed even, reminding her of the time she broke her personal best in the 880 run. The way her legs had shaken the entire bus trip back had frightened her. The coach had kept urging her to drink more and eat a banana. She was sure she hadn't run any races now, but she might have. Pressing her fingers into her leg muscles didn't stop the trembling.

"Ah, the shakes usually accompany torture." He stretched out his arm as if to touch her.

Leah jerked back, lost her balance, and fell backward to slam her head against the floor. She lay for a moment with her eyes closed. Could she possibly play dead? Numerous people talked about surviving the Holocaust by pretending to be dead. It might work for her. Breathing in deeply, she held her breath. How long it would take to convince her captor she'd expired?

The sound of the chair scraping against the wood as the man stood indicated her performance lacked some authenticity. She heard the rustle of his robes along with his accompanying footsteps. Leah willed herself not to move, *to hold perfectly still. Actors did it in movies all the time. Why couldn't she?*

His shadow loomed over her, touching her. "Oh, Arabella," he said softly.

She'd hoped believing she was dead, he might feel some regret for treating her so poorly. A metallic sound echoed off the wall. Her head snapped off the ground, bowing her back into a curve with agonizing pain to her neck, forcing out a gasp as her eyes flickered open. He held a short chain in his hands attached to a cool metal band that encompassed her neck.

Pulling her slowly back into a sitting position, he dropped the chain. "Arabella, you could never fool me, a lesson that never took. You used to call me your own beloved Lionel, but now you pretend we have never met."

It was an intimate matter. Hard to imagine there was anything to love about this malevolent bag of bones, but perhaps there had been at one time.

Should she flatter the man? Tell him how she missed him? Pretend to recognize him?

The decision vanished as she found herself in the rolling chair beside her friend in the county library.

CHAPTER SEVEN

S TELLA SPUN AROUND, looking both relieved and angry. "There
you're! I checked the aisles, the restroom, even asked the reference
librarian. I wasn't even sure how I would get home if I couldn't find
you. I called your phone, but it was here." She angled her head in the
direction of the bright lime-green cell phone lying by the keyboard.
"Where have you been?"

Leah listened patiently to her friend's rant, holding herself up with
one arm resting on the counter. "I think you're going to have to drive. I
don't feel so well."

Her friend placed her hand against her forehead. "Your skin is
clammy. I'll drive you home, but I doubt your father will be too
pleased."

She tried to push her lips into a smile but failed. "Just don't kill us."
Stella tried to help her up, but staggered under her weight.

The helpful reference librarian came to assist. "What's wrong with
her?"

"Some type of brain fever or malaria," Stella offered. Leah wished
she'd be quiet. Unlike most teenagers, lying to adults was a skill her
friend lacked, not that she was much better. Still, she knew enough not
to make the mistake of elaborating too much, as Stella often did.

"Really?" The doubt was obvious in the librarian's voice. "I considered that more of a tropical disease."

Leah could hear one of the patrons murmuring something about a strung-out junkie. The man was talking about her. The nerve. Just went to show what happened when you made assumptions. She wanted to march back to them and explain that she'd just shifted through centuries and been tortured by thugs for something she couldn't remember doing. Of course, that would only confirm his earlier junkie assessment with such outrageous claims.

Stella opened her mouth. A tale including missionary parents and malaria emerged. Great, just her luck the librarian would ask her parents about their religious outreach when they visited the library next. Her mother would politely tell her she didn't believe in inflicting her religious beliefs on others and would promptly hand her a pamphlet on how to help Mother Earth.

Her eyelids flickered shut as her butt hit the car upholstery. "Keys in pocket." She pushed out the words.

Leah retained consciousness, but she wished she hadn't. The way her friend drove, going up on curbs only to careen back down with a jolt, rattled her brain even more. A cacophony of horns indicated either Stella had stolen a right-of-way or had run a red light. Leah bet it was the former.

The sedan bumped into the driveway, where Stella laid on the horn, bringing out Leah's father, followed by her mother and ever-curious brother. Having reached her limit, her friend babbled as her father opened the driver's side door. "Please help Leah. She went away and then came back. She can barely walk."

Her father hurried to Leah's side of the car. She recognized his voice. How would she explain? He scooped her up in his arms and carried her into the house. Sometimes she forgot how strong he could be until needed. "What has happened?"

She opened her mouth to reply, but her father kept talking. "I hope you did not get in a fight where someone films it and puts it up on the

Internet."

Ethan bounced along beside them, opening the front door wide. "Get real, Dad. Stella and Leah are not the type to start girl fights."

Mother hovered close by smoothing her hair. The pinched expression on her mother's face concerned her. She tried to spare her mother grief by not telling her things. She'd not mentioned that their various moves made it hard to fit in at school. Her brother thought he knew it all, but he was unaware she'd been in three girl fights due to being the new kid.

Being new was enough to set some people off. The early altercations had taught her to go in ruthless. Acting insane didn't hurt, either. That should have been her tactic with her medieval tormenter.

Nana pushed her way to Leah's side. "My poor dear, did you travel back in time again?"

She blinked her eyes twice for yes since her throat was too raw for talking.

As her father carried her to bed, her mother's voice rose above everyone else's. It was a tone seldom used by her mother and never when speaking to her opinionated mother. "What do you mean, traveling back in time?"

Her mother's irritation most likely resulted from Leah telling Nana about the time travel as opposed to her. She could hear her grandmother's efforts to calm her mother, which was definitely a turn of the tables.

Her father knelt to place her on the bed. Theodora jumped up beside her and began to knead her stomach, causing her to whimper.

Both Nana and Mother stopped their fussing to look over at her. Their faces were white, bodies frozen, until Leah whimpered again, causing them both to spring like racehorses out of the gate. Mother reached her first and shoved her father aside, but Nana moved fast for a woman with a cane. When they peeled back the shirt sticking to her skin, the two gasped. Pushing up on her elbows, she was able to see the crisscross marks on her torso.

"Damn delinquents." Her father growled the words. "I'm calling the police."

"Wait." Nana's imperious tone cut through the tension enveloping the room. "Only thing that will come of that is they will lock you up for child abuse and send in some social worker who will have Leah removed to some dubious foster family who might actually abuse her. Do you want that?"

A frown pulled at his lips as he crossed his arms. "No, I don't want that. What can we do? She needs to go to a hospital."

"Adam." Her mother touched her father's arm. "I'm almost done with my clinicals. I can take care of her here. At the hospital, she'd get the same treatment plus a call to social services. A whipped victim would receive an automatic referral, which would put us back right to the same place."

Leah forced her eyes open as she watched her family discuss her as if she were an uninterested third party. Yep, her unplanned trips to the past would be hard to explain to any social worker or cop. They'd not only have her family up on abuse charges, but might lock her away in some psych ward. Just the other day, her biggest problem had been getting Dylan to notice her. If only she could turn back the clock.

Nana and Mother exchanged a few words and then hurried off in different directions, leaving Stella and Ethan to gaze at her as if she were a two-headed cow. Their wordless scrutiny made her uncomfortable.

In hopes of breaking the tension, she looked up at her friend. "Not exactly what you were expecting from a trip to the library?" she joked.

"No." Stella shook her head, speaking slowly, no doubt searching for the right words. "In a way, I guess it is a real-life example of religious persecution."

Leah tried for a smile but even her face hurt. "We should get an A on our report for going the extra mile, or three thousand miles. I'm not sure it is about religion. Hard to say. I think it is a love affair gone bad. People always say something is about religion to justify their bad behavior, especially if it is a popular opinion."

Dad stood next to the door with his arms still folded and his brow furrowed, probably chafing at his inability to do anything. "Sounds like you're getting a bit philosophical."

Leah speared her fingers through her hair. "I'm not sure. I guess things aren't always as they seem on the surface. The people I've met in the past are motivated by fear and greed." The trio of Henry, Sabina, and Margaret had run out of fear. What about the villagers? It would have been easy to assume some moral high ground motivated them. They could even tell themselves that as they turned on their neighbors.

Her father's thoughts must have mirrored her own. "In the end, you have to think did turning on their neighbors benefit them? The same person they vilified may have helped with the harvest only months ago. At first, they do nothing out of fear, not wanting to attract attention. Then again, what benefit is it to them? Do they get the goods or land of the persecuted individual?"

Sabina had complained the women disliked her because she was attractive and unmarried. "They might get rid of the competition for the affection of a beau or even a husband."

Leah imagined there were definitely a few women in the village who wouldn't mind seeing the beautiful woman disappear, and they wouldn't care how it happened.

Ethan grimaced. "Girls, They're even mean in the past."

"Yeah," Leah agreed. "You have no clue, little brother. Be glad you're a male. All you guys do is punch each other in the nose when you get aggravated, then suddenly you're pals."

Her brother's hand went up to feel his nose. "I don't want to be punched in the nose again." He displayed some concern about the future of his nose and some puzzlement as to why someone might want to rearrange it. Keeping his hand protectively over his nose, he left the room, passing Nana and Mother on their way in. They laid out the homemade bandages that had cartoon images on them. The old, faded sheet set from her younger years finally been put to a different use.

Mother carried a teakettle with a plume of steam wafting gently behind her as she walked. Leah looked at the teakettle, while hoping boiling water didn't constitute a cure for anything.

"BOILING WATER AND torn-up sheets. Is not this what they always ask for when someone is having a baby?"

Setting the kettle down, her mother shooed her father from the room, turning to a swaying Stella, she asked, "Would you like to help?"

Her answer was a soft, "I guess."

Nana took the lid off a pot that held an aromatic mixture. "Old family secret that will heal your wounds in no time." She shoved the pot in Stella's direction, causing her to stagger a few steps back.

Her mother poured the hot water into a dishpan and began to dip some of the bandages in it. "We may have to soften up your clothes to separate them from your wounds. Pulling them off would only cause the scabs to break open."

Her mother went about her duties with a no-nonsense attitude, which was probably her approach at work. The idea of tearing open scabbed-over wounds caused Leah to shudder. She'd never been a good patient. She'd made it her life mission not to do dangerous things when she'd relatives who were more likely to pull out a needle and put in a few stitches after splashing her with alcohol. Nope, she'd stayed away from anything even slightly dangerous, from skateboarding to rollerblading.

Ironic that now she'd to endure pretty much everything she'd avoided.

Even though the water had to have been burning, her mother calmly wrung out the bandages and placed them against her shirt. Steeling herself for the pain by tightening her muscles, Leah felt slow warmth penetrate the fabric, skin, and eventually her muscles, relaxing her. Her eyelids fluttered shut as her mother placed several more warm bandages around her torso.

With her eyes closed, she felt safe listening to her mother and grandmother talk to each other as they moved around her. Her friend asked a few halting, difficult-to-hear questions. Her grandmother gave her the usual cryptic answers she seemed to have for everything that often appeared to answer the question, but on deeper inspection said nothing at all.

Her mother bent over her body, removing the cooling bandages. "I'm going to remove your shirt. I hope it is not a favorite, because I'm going to cut it off you." Flourishing a pair of blunt-nosed scissors, she eased the tip of the metal shears under the material and snipped, pulling the fabric gently away. Nana hovered over her mother, leaning on her cane, probably anxious to offer instruction, but for once, she held her tongue.

Her mother's gasp broke through her stupor. What was it? She saw the blue polo she'd donned earlier that day in strips around her torso. Make that, her striped torso. Her body was a quilt of yellowing, blue and black bruises separated by red lash marks crusting over with pus and dried blood. Not a pretty sight, and apparently, she wasn't the only one who felt that way. Stella darted out of the room with a hand over her mouth, making a retching noise.

The soft sound of Nana's chanting as she moved above her, holding out her hands to invoke a healing protection spell, both frightened and reassured Leah. The words sounded foreign to her, probably Romany. In times of great distress, Nana often abandoned speaking in English, claiming it took too much thought when all one could do was feel. How serious was it that Nana brought out the language of her ancestors? In another way, it reassured her. Nana wasn't above murmuring a few Gypsy words to give her paying customers the feeling they had an authentic fortune-teller. Of course, that was all for show. Leah knew this time the words were not for show, but were serious business, which unfortunately was her business.

Her mother's arms wrapped around her as if in an embrace, pulling her slightly forward. Leah lifted her hands to her mother's arms. How long since they had truly hugged? She could not remember. It wasn't that she disliked her mother. Hugging fell about the wayside, along with evening bed-tucks. After all, she was almost a senior. Too old for such things, they said, "I love you," or "Love you, too," at the end of conversations. It often felt meaningless, rather like a clerk wishing her a nice day with a snarl in her voice. She leaned into her mother's arms, taking solace from the simple action.

The brief embrace lasted only seconds, until her mother whispered in her ear, "I need you to try to sit up on your own so I can cut off the shirt from your back."

Was that all it had been? Not a hug, not a sign of love, but only a way to get to her back to cut her shirt off? Leah didn't want to consider it. Of course, her mother loved her. That's what mothers did. Instead, she willed herself to hold her body erect during the process of the cool metal medical shears moving down her back. Would it be too much to ask for reassurance of her love?

Her mother's voice, clouded with concern, breathed on her neck. "You do realize that if there was a way, I would take your place. I love you, Leah. Nana has explained to me this is your journey, but that doesn't mean I have to like it."

Leah allowed her head to drop to her mother's shoulder. Resting it there, she inhaled her familiar scent of lily of the valley perfume, wondering if this could be the last conversation between the two of them. "That makes two of us. I love you, too." She mumbled her reply but knew her mother heard.

Her grandmother picked up a paintbrush and stirred the pot.

"You're using a paintbrush on me?" What was she, a house?

Her mother cleaned her back as Nana drew closer. "A paintbrush will help provide the solution in an even fashion. Yes, there's much of you that needs to be covered."

Her mother unsnapped her bra. Realizing the action might reveal more marks and require a total stripping had something rising up in her throat, gagging her some. She swallowed as her mother swiped down her bra-strap area.

"This area is clean."

The announcement relieved her some. It was worst when she could not remember what had happened.

The smooth slide of the brush on her back was warm and moist, and it smelled strongly of garlic. As it brushed over her wounds, it stung. Probably salt or vinegar in the mixture. Better than alcohol, she reminded herself, and fought against wincing.

"Sit up straight," her mother urged.

Her changed posture allowed her mother and grandmother to work as a tag team, with Nana spreading the unguent while Mother wrapped bandages around her torso. With her upper torso and arms done, her head was lowered to the pillow to rest before they tackled her lower body. It made her feel a bit like a pharaoh being prepared for burial. Of course, they were dead at the time. Still, they were familiar with the process. Closing her eyes, she decided to take a tiny break with no intention of sleeping. When she slept, her mind wandered often into the other century.

✧   ✧   ✧

IT WAS A warm spring day. A few trees sported blossoms, while others wore new leaves. Birds called to each other in a mating ritual, hoping to find a mate before nesting began. The sun was shining, and she was done with her morning chores. A sense of freedom assailed her as she ran down the hill as fast as her young legs could propel her. Her laughter floated out behind her, as did her homespun skirt.

Reaching the flat land, she spun in circles. Her dull, circle skirt flared out. She'd asked her mother if they could dye their clothes magnificent colors, such as the red and purple of the spring flowers. Her mother had said those colors were not for them. It did not make sense to her. If flowers could wear such vivid colors, why not people?

She pretended not to see him hiding among the trees. Her brother teased her that Lionel, the lord's third son, had feelings for her. Even at ten, she knew the ways of men and women. Being married at twelve, while not common, wasn't rare, either. She needed to look to her future, and Lionel might be that future.

He stepped out from behind the trees and approached with a determined gait. "Ho, Arabella, well met," he called out, as if he'd happened to meet her while walking, as opposed to waiting for her.

She smiled sweetly, her eyes sparkling at the coltish boy. He was handsome with his unmarked skin and thick, brown hair. "Good day, Lionel." Feeling unusually daring, she added, "My beloved Lionel."

His smile was reward enough, but from behind his back, he brought out a fistful of half-wilted wildflowers. "For you."

She took the flowers and held them up to her nose. Why did her father discourage her association with Lionel? He was kind to her. In time, he might even be lord of the manor. How could such an association be wrong?

They walked side by side under the warming sun. Saying nothing, Lionel reached for her hand, and she allowed him to take it, intertwining their fingers.

"Arabella," he started, his smile vanishing while his fingers tightened. "I'm going to have to go away for schooling. I should have left years ago, but my mother begged my father to let me stay since I was the last of her other sons left at home. Reginald is away at school, while Archibald fosters at another household."

Schooling. She'd heard of it. It was something males did. Wellborn males. Boys like her brother took up the father's trade or were fortunate to be an apprentice to a tradesman. "Where is this school?"

Her heart made a little lurch as if it knew her life was about to change. There were some in the village who had made mention of how her mother thought too much of herself and put on airs, and as the daughter of such a woman, she was twice as bad. Her mother had assured her that such women spoke out of spite. They were not as well favored nor were their daughters.

Their hands still united, pulled her to a stop with him. Facing her, his dark eyes held hers. "Arabella, I know not where this school is. Know this. I will come back for you." He dropped a kiss on her hair from his superior height.

"I will wait," she promised, determined to do just that, despite her initial reluctance.

Later that day, she confided to her brother that Lionel had to go away to schooling. Her brother shook his head, muttering something about Lionel becoming a dress wearer.

"Tomas, you make no sense," she complained.

"Little sister, it is time for you to look elsewhere for a mate. Lionel is too high for you, but even if he does care for you, as the third son, he's for the church. Since his family has popish ways, they will turn him into a skirt-wearing Jesuit. No wife or women in his life from now on." Her brother *shook his head, giving her a sad smile as he headed for the barn.*

"He told me to wait," she shouted after him.

Her mother, carrying a double-bucket yoke, met her on the path. "Who are you supposed to wait for?"

"Lionel," she explained, knowing she'd an avid supporter in her mother. "Tomas tells me he will be a skirt-wearing priest who will take no wife."

Her mother's still beautiful face took on a reflective mien. "Ah, 'tis so. I suspected otherwise since his mother held on to him so long. Ye best be looking. Make haste as well, as the other girls have sized up the available men while ye been making cow eyes at Lionel."

She wanted to argue. Her mother had encouraged their association, but now everything had changed. Marriage of daughters helped to forge helpful connections. Her family was a moderate one in the village, not too poor, but not over-rich. Her father could cobble together a decent dowry, but her older sister, Helena, needed to marry fast. At fourteen, she was on her way to earning the labels of old and persnickety.

Lionel hadn't even left, and yet his abandonment weighed heavy on her.

✧ ✧ ✧

A GENTLE ROCKING woke her. She blinked twice and stared into Nana's face. "Did you drift way to the other time?"

Leah blinked, slowly allowing the room to come into focus, allowing her thoughts time to coalesce. "I'm not sure. I may have just remembered something from the past. I understand now why Lionel hates me, or I should say Arabella, so much."

Nana stroked her cheek with her age-freckled hand. "Why is that, sweet pea?"

"He asked her to wait for him while he went away to priest school. Arabella's family advised against it, pointing out she'd miss getting a good husband. Nana, she was only ten. How should she know what to do at that age?" It seemed unfair to expect a ten-year-old to make life-altering decisions.

"Keep in mind that to live to be forty was average for the women. To be an elderly woman was another sign the witch hunters used to point out association with the devil. I'd say it was a sign of lack of association with men in general, since most women died in childbirth or from the difficulties resulting from a birth. It was a hard life for a woman. Yes, Lionel would have expected her to wait. Women generally did what men told them to do. It would be enough of a reason for him to want revenge, especially if he loved her." Nana limped toward her dresser to pour a glass of water.

Her grandmother lurched a little without the cane, sloshing the water she'd poured. Even if the glass were half full, she'd accept it gratefully. The image of Arabella's self-serving attitude was bitter in her memory. Why would a man like such a little brat? Apparently, he'd come back but had not found her waiting. Where had she gone? Why had Lionel felt the need to ring retribution on the entire village?

CHAPTER EIGHT

A LONG, PIERCING scream jolted Leah wake. Had she fallen asleep again? She hadn't meant to. Where was she? It was dark. Who screamed? The gentle purr of Theodora reassured her, along with the glowing red numerals of her clock radio. The sound of tire wheels screeching and her brother shouting, "Floor it, they're getting away!" emphasized it was a normal Thursday with her father and brother indulging in their love of crime dramas.

Who would have thought such things would offer comfort? Occasionally, the local paper would run stories about teens helping in Third World countries or after natural disasters. The central theme was how grateful they'd become for what they had after such an experience. Usually, they joked about things like cell phones, hair dryers, or the Internet. There was so much more to miss, such as basic laws to prevent your neighbor from burning your house down and trying to do likewise to you.

Pushing up in her bed, she gathered a few pillows to plump behind her back and placed Theodora in her lap. The cat promptly curled herself into a circle and began purring. Leah scratched the feline's head as she pondered what made people act in horrific ways.

Some experts would say it was because the villagers were uneducated and easily manipulated by their fear, which was true to an extent. Leah had experienced enough mean-girl spite to want to avoid it, but she certainly didn't consider herself ignorant. Centuries later, people still resorted to genocide, while ethnic groups had been living in harmony, often intermarrying, until one charismatic and driven individual decided it was wrong.

Miss Santiago had explained how throughout history there seemed to be a need for an enemy for people to hate. Politicians, ministers, and advertisers capitalized on it. The enemy kept changing. Americans used to hate the Brits. Now, they were übercool, especially their accents. Before she'd been born, the Russians were bad news. They, too, had morphed into some sort of distant neighbor who was both mysterious and intriguing.

Depending on which group you belonged to, you hated the Jews, the gays, the Democrats, or anyone who didn't claim to be a Christian. The general impression was that different was bad and dangerous. Leah sighed. The more things changed, the more they stayed the same. In a high school of more than three thousand students, the majority of them tried to be the same.

The school did its part by issuing uniforms. Even if it hadn't, a uniform policy would have happened in a more insidious fashion. The popular crowd would have set the fashion tone, and those who could copy it would. Those who chose not to or couldn't afford the brands, would earn sly insults that sometimes sounded like compliments, but everyone would know better. Without fashions to comment on, the popular crowd liked to ridicule the actual bodies wearing the clothing. No one ever came out well, either.

The door cracked, letting in light as her mother peeped in. "You're awake."

"Yeah."

Leah's sister, Nora, always joked that their mother stated the obvious, which was often true. Her mother slipped into the room, leaving the door slightly ajar. Yellow light spilled in, a slice highlighting her wood floor, leaving the rest of the room in shadows.

Her mother smoothed out a place on her bed before perching on the edge. "Could you use some company?"

Nora would have pointed out to their mother that she'd already taken a seat before she asked the question. "Yes, I could use some company." It would be nice to have conversations that made sense instead of cryptic inferences to a past she did not remember.

Her mother patted her leg under the cover. "I miss talking with you. I know part of it is my fault because I'm gone so much with work and school, but I do remember when we used to sit and talk."

"Me, too." The image of them sitting around the kitchen table preparing a meal and chatting came to mind. They used to work together to prepare supper. Even Ethan had contributed. Somehow, that had slipped away as their schedules changed, and they'd started eating more sandwiches and pizza. "When did that stop?"

"I'd say about four years ago. The same time I decided I wanted to be a nurse. I knew there would be sacrifices to get there, but I didn't realize it would mean cutting out our time." Her voice stumbled on the last two words.

The darkness made it hard to distinguish whether her mother was close to tears or just tired. "It's still our time. Anything you want to talk about?"

Her mother forced a laugh. "Tons. What were you thinking about when I came in?"

Leah's hand stilling on Theodora caused the feline to turn her head into her palm, her way of insisting the petting continue. Message noted, she continued to stroke the cat. "I was trying to figure out why people tend to hate people that are different. Why the kids in our school are so anxious to conform to whatever is the accepted norm even if they think it is BS? Why does it matter if someone is different?"

Her mother's hand tightened on her leg for a second. "It really doesn't matter if people are different. It's preferable. Can you imagine if everyone were pianists? There'd be no one to play the violin, fix your car, or examine your sick child. Currently, there's a perception that to be different is wrong. The people who resist being different have some strange agenda that usually makes sense only to them. Think about ancient times, when people worshipped several deities at once. You might have been friends with a person who followed Zeus, while you were an Artemis devotee."

The image of Stella and a few other friends in togas amused her. "It's like that with music. A few friends like country, others jazz, and still others classical, and yet we can still talk. I probably wouldn't want to go to a concert with them. Then again, maybe I would just for the experience."

"It does my heart good to hear you say such a thing. Makes me think your father and I did something right." Her voice had started low and melodious. It grew a little thin at the end, as if she was fighting back emotions.

Pushing Theodora out of her lap, Leah bent toward her mother and opened her arms. They embraced, with Leah resting her head on her mother's shoulder. "You guys did a lot right. The fact I don't feel the need to hate any group is a major point in your favor."

Her mother tightened the hug. It didn't hurt. Leah stretched her fingers and toes and flexed her muscles, causing her mother to ask, "What are you doing?"

"Just checking. Nothing hurts anymore. I think I'm well enough to go to school tomorrow." Leah knew she was weird. She actually wanted to go to school. For the most part, she liked it. What else was she going to do? Hanging around watching daytime television was not an option. Thinking of school reminded her of her friend. "What happened to

Stella?"

Her mother released her and leaned back on her hands. "Oh, your father had to drive her home." In the dim light, her exaggerated expression of rolled eyes and wry smile were visible. "I imagine he debriefed her about jumping centuries, magickal healing elixirs, and such. He has a way of making the oddest things sound believable. He convinced me, right? A witch married to a Bible-thumper."

Leah never thought of her father as being persuasive. He certainly was intelligent and rational. It made her wonder what types of conversations her parents had had. Still harder for her to understand was why her father had knowingly dated a witch. "Maybe he thought he'd convert you."

"I doubt that." Her mother shook her head. "We never talked of religion, his or mine. We never even…"

"Hold that thought," Leah warned. "I want to think of you as my parents, not some rebellious, wild college students who did things I don't want to hear about."

Her mother's laughter washed over her, light and lilting. "Leah, Leah, you're being silly. You don't want to hear about how your father and I were crazy mad in love? All we could think of was when we'd be together next. When we were together, we made love so passionate the Love Goddess applauded us."

"Mom," Leah pretended to complain. "Please, you're traumatizing me."

Her mother bounced on the bed a little, overcome with mirth. Leaning forward, she touched Leah's shoulder. "You know, we still do."

"Ugh." Leah covered her ears. This wasn't news to her, since it was a small house, but she pretended to be astounded. "Years of therapy in my future."

Her mother pried her hands off her ears. "Listen, sweetie. I want the same for you. It could happen."

"Yeah, but there's this issue with staying in the same century. What if I meet someone when I'm in the past?" Not like that was going to happen, since most of them weren't big on bathing. They also had all those rules about what women couldn't do, which was pretty much everything except cooking, keeping house, and having babies.

"I've thought about this. This jumping back and forth in time is new to me. I've never known anyone doing it, but I've read about it. You have a mission to accomplish. Most of us get to work out our destiny in our own century, but you're special."

"Yay special," Leah mock cheered.

"It makes me wonder if there's something only you can do. No one in that time will suffice. Could be there's someone you're supposed to meet. If so, I would prefer they'd be here in a new version in this century, too. That's the mother in me talking. I've heard of people passing into other times and staying."

Leah's heart leaped. She even pinched herself with her ragged fingernails to make sure she was not dreaming. It would have to be a dream if her mother spoke utter nonsense. "What? Are you kidding me?"

"While you were sleeping, darling, I've been doing some research. It's difficult. There's the issue of, if a person stays in the past, they will never be born in the future, which means people won't remember they existed."

The words tumbled out in a rush, as if she were anxious to push them out or run them by her fast enough she'd not make sense of them, but Leah understood perfectly. She speared one hand through her hair, which felt dirty and greasy, as if she hadn't washed it for days. Yuk, somehow she was already going medieval. "Wait. You think other people disappeared into time, but we don't have any records of it because no one remembered them once they disappeared? Is that about it?"

"Pretty much. Still, the universe places us where we're needed, and right now, it needs you in the past."

Her mother spoke the statement with a mixture of acceptance and bafflement. Probably the same way the ancient Mayan sacrifices had spoken of knowing they were about to be killed and considered it an honor? Wait a minute. She'd be the sacrifice, not her mother. That would make her mother...the mother of the sacrifice.

"I don't want to go in the past or serve a purpose."

Wrapping her fingers around hers, her mother squeezed her hand. "I don't want you to go, either. So far, there doesn't seem to be any way to stop it."

That's what she'd thought. Didn't parents rush in and save their children from things that might hurt them? Goddess knows, her family had tried. Her father had disassembled their metal swing set after she'd taken a header from the sliding board. The swing set hadn't caused the accident. She'd tried to fly.

All the cartoon witches could fly. She'd figured she should have been able to fly, too. She'd never confessed why she'd fallen. She hadn't wanted her family to know she'd failed at being a witch. Often, she'd wondered if she were their natural child. Failure to fly had confirmed her adoption status. "You know I used to think I was adopted, just some ordinary child without parents you picked up one day."

"Really?" Her mother's voice reflected surprise. "You resembled Nora, and were little like me, but you're the mirror image of your grandmother when she was sixteen."

"I never saw any photos of Nana when she was young."

There had been a few in the last ten years. Nana would commandeer the camera and shoot photos, but seldom, if ever, would she be in them. In some ways, she resembled some suspicious tribesman convinced the camera would steal her soul. Her grandmother might have been on the run from the law, too.

Her mother fingered the covers. "My mother stopped appearing in pictures about the same time my father disappeared."

Her grandfather had vanished? She'd always assumed he'd died. There was an understanding among all of them that no mention was ever made of his name. Early on, when she'd started kindergarten and the other children had had grandfathers show up for Grandparents' Day, she'd made the mistake of asking where hers was. Nana had locked herself in her room for the duration of the day with a brandy bottle. The sound of soft sobbing had slipped under the door, which had confused Leah. Nana never cried. Her mother had explained that her grandfather was gone, which she assumed was a euphemism for dead.

Among the other students, a few divorced grandmas had used words like horn-dog and old codger to refer to the missing grandfather. Her mother had shushed her, asking her to never repeat the words. If her grandparents had divorced, she'd no doubt Nana would have had even more colorful names for her grandfather. All she really knew was his name had been Buell. Her mother's voice interrupted her musings, making her wonder how long she'd been talking.

"Before he disappeared, your grandfather was the love of your grandmother's life. Of course, I always thought of them as old since they were my parents, but they weren't, not really. He was as old as your father is now when he went missing. Before that, they were always laughing, playing, even dancing around the house. Nana loved to take photos. Ironically, it was usually her and Dad mugging for the camera. She called him her soul mate, swore she'd searched lifetimes to find him, and to lose him again devastated her. For a few years, I worried she'd never snap out of her depression, but then Nora was born, which started her living again."

A man disappearing off the face of the earth without a sign was a bit bizarre. It sounded like one of those crime shows, except Grandpa would not have been a sexy young woman trusting the wrong people in her effort to be a star. "Didn't you look for him?"

"We did. Called the police, for all the good it did us. They implied he was a grown man who could go where he pleased, and it pleased him to be elsewhere. Nana called in the Pagan community. We did physical searches, posted missing signs, ran ads in the newspaper and on the Internet. Several times that year, Nana went down to the coroner to look at unclaimed bodies fitting my father's description. They weren't him. The search took its toll on her. Eventually she took down all the pictures of him around the house and packed up his clothes." Her mother's voice grew hoarse as she wiped a tear away.

Such a disappearance smelled of foul play or even magick. "Do you think he could have been the victim of a hex or magick gone wrong?"

Sniffling, she shook her head, coughed, and then cleared her throat. "You never knew my father, but there was no one he wouldn't help. He was a jolly fellow, joking with the men, complimenting the women, and playing with the children. He'd to be one of the best-loved men in town. No one would have wanted to hurt him. No one."

"Do you think," Leah hesitated not wanting to give false hope to an old sorrow, "he fell into a time portal?"

Twisting her hair around her finger, she sat, saying nothing for a few seconds. "Maybe."

"If so, what about your theory that no one would remember you if you went back in time?" Leah feared she might have raised hope only to dash it down again.

"Well, uh," her mother started, then looked off to the dark corner. She spoke slowly, more as if she were thinking aloud as opposed to talking to Leah. "I've never known anyone who traveled to the past, except for you. My theory is not much of a theory, because it hasn't been tested."

Actually, it had. Leah realized she was the official time-traveling guinea pig. "It has been tested. I tested it in the last forty-eight hours. Did you ever think you only had two children?" The concept of a person vanishing in a second from the memories of everyone who knew her was staggering. What if for a few moments, her mother really did forget her? Then again, if she came back, wouldn't she bring back the memory of herself to all who knew her?

The sound of another car chase carried down the hall and into her room. She couldn't accuse the males in her family of having intellectual television choices. Her mother steepled her fingers and stared into a dark corner. "I can't remember thinking I only had two kids. Could this be because you keep coming back?"

It was the same thought she'd had, but it didn't answer anything. "I don't know what it means. I wonder if it's like a movie I saw once where all those who died went to a city to live, not unlike any other city, with stores, restaurants, and apartments. As long as people remembered them, they continued to exist, but when people forgot them, they began to fade until they were no more. Your father is like that. He exists because you remember him."

Theodora bumped against her, signaling she was tired of people ignoring her. Leah picked up the feline and cuddled her a little. Too bad people couldn't be more like cats and demanded simply what they needed. When someone ignored them, they went to someone else. Eventually, cats got what they wanted.

The slice of light on the floor widened as Nana pushed the door open. "What are you girls doing sitting in the dark?"

Leah's mother turned to the door and motioned her in. "Come in. We're thinking and theorizing. We've come up with something to consider."

Nana entered the room, using her cane to sweep in front of her as if she were blind. Leah realized the low light must have made it difficult for her to see, but then she decided her grandmother was mocking her lack of tidiness. "It's not that messy."

Nana reached her bed and eased down on the foot of it. "I never said it was. Makes me wonder why you're so touchy."

It was better not to debate with Nana. The woman was smarter than anyone she'd ever met, which humbled her, since Nana had never finished high school. The school of hard knocks and an internship at the University of Experience taught Nana all she needed to know. All the same, she'd a feeling her grandmother would not enjoy their sudden insight into what may have happened to her husband.

"Mother, Leah and I were talking about her sojourns into another century. While she was gone, none of us had a sense of her not with us. We didn't forget her when she physically left us." Her speech slowed as if she wasn't sure of her thoughts or was afraid of mentioning her father.

Nana nodded. "I agree. Never forget my Leah." She reached out to pat her legs outlined by the covers. "Maura, what is your point? I know you must have one, or you wouldn't have bothered with this long, rambling introduction."

"I do." Her head swung to Leah, who nodded a little to encourage her mother to continue. "What if father slipped into another time?"

"Maura." Nana's voice grew stronger as she pushed herself up from the bed. "You know better than to speak of your father. You're just being cruel."

"Wait," Leah called, surprised that she'd be the one to try to make her headstrong grandmother listen. "I know it hurts, but what if Grandfather somehow fell into a different time? I've proved it's possible."

Nana swayed a little as she planted her cane for support. "It could be possible. If so, why doesn't he come back?"

Her mother shrugged. Her grandmother seemed to deflate in front of her. It was up to her to do something. "Maybe he can't. It's not a problem of wanting. I never try to go, but then I'm there. When I'm there, I'm usually talking to someone when I disappear again. Guess that won't do much for my witch reputation."

Nana appeared to think about what she'd said and made two halting steps to the bed, where she eased herself down again. "I assume there was another you there, which allows you to join and leave at will. For Buell, there's only one him, which keeps him there."

Her mother reached for her grandmother's hand. "Dad used to be able to predict better than you."

"Oh yes," she agreed. "All he'd to do is touch someone's hand, and he could tell their future. Other times, just their name was enough."

Leah watched the exchange between the two. She thought she knew where her mother was going.

"What if Dad fell through a portal? He even sought it out because he knew it was part of his destiny," her mother suggested matter-of-factly.

Yep, only in her family did people casually pass through centuries and regard it as fate. Did non-magickal people pass through time and slowly lose their minds due to their inability to accept such a transition? She accepted it, but it was far from easy, especially knowing she could disappear into the past at any time. It sucked, since she almost had things worked out in this century. Not perfect, but she was getting there.

Emotions shifted across her grandmother's face in such a rapid sequence it was hard to catalog them all, but the last one appeared to be hope. "It would be like Buell not to tell me, afraid I might stop him, which I would have, if only to keep him selfishly to myself."

Leah had never seen such vulnerability before, at least on Nana's face. This woman put fear into high school administrators. "He could have gone ahead to be in place to help me."

"That's it." Nana stamped her cane in agitation. "That's exactly what Buell did."

What had she done? The only reason she'd suggested it was because her grandmother had suddenly appeared as fragile as a glass vase teetering on the edge of the table. She didn't think she'd take her seriously. Her mother's contented smile signaled she, too, believed her off-the-wall suggestion.

Great, now everyone believed her. When had she graduated to fortune-teller? Wasn't it enough to try to find a way to convince Lionel she was not the girl who'd jilted him? Now she'd to bring Grandfather back with her, or everyone would be disappointed. She'd never ever seen a picture of him. How would she recognize him if she did stumble across him?

CHAPTER NINE

THE ALARM JOLTED her awake as usual. Leah pushed herself out of bed, wondering why her legs wouldn't bend well. A quick downward glance revealed her bandages. A fading memory of being beaten flickered in her mind. A beating should stay in a person's mind, but it hadn't. Once she'd left the other century, the memories had grown faint. How was she going to succeed if she couldn't remember? Would she have to repeat the same thing over and over again? It was a good chance her body might not hold up to another beating.

A nearby notebook collected her dreams as she wrote down all she could remember, including the image of her and Lionel as childhood sweethearts. Was Arabella a mean girl of her time? What was normal by her time standards could appear mean in this century. The girl tried to make the best of her circumstances. Her writing was almost illegible as she filled several pages with her big, loopy writing. She could read it, but she might be the only person. She could type it later.

It might be a good record, in case she never returned. Not exactly a cheerful thought, but someone should know her story. The second alarm went off, reminding her she only had fifteen minutes to get ready for school. Dropping her notebook, she managed to locate a clean pair of pants and a polo top. Another quick search netted her panties and a bra. Her room could benefit from cleaning.

Her parents and Nana sat at the kitchen table, talking. Odd, but no one was hurrying to get ready for work. Ethan popped out of his room, still wearing his cartoon pajamas. That was going to put a clog in everything if her brother wasn't ready. His bus would arrive before she left for school since he was bussed across town. Eyeing him suspiciously, she inquired, "You're not sick, are you?"

"No, we're all staying home today just in case you disappear again. It might be my last time to see my big sister." Ethan startled her enough to allow him time to dart into the bathroom before she could. Was he making it up? She hadn't put it past her brother.

Giving up on having access to the bathroom anytime soon, she walked into the kitchen. Maps, large reference books, and a few photographs of a younger Nana looking adoringly at a grinning, dark-haired man littered the kitchen table. No one had to tell her she was finally seeing a picture of her grandfather when he'd been very young. Her grandmother had looked surprisingly like her. She picked up the photograph and cradled it in her hands.

The man had an open, trusting face with wide-set eyes and dark, backswept hair. He reminded her of Dylan a little, not so much in looks, but more in attitude. This man had loved life. Life had done him the courtesy of loving him right back. Even though her grandmother's face was turned so she could look at him, it was obvious she adored him. What must it be like to be that much in love? Wow, she hoped she lived long enough to find out. It also helped her to understand the depth of Nana's sorrow.

Leah carefully placed the photo back on the table, she caught her grandmother looking expectantly at her. Nana waited for her to say something, so she did. "He certainly was a handsome fellow. He looks like he was a friend to everyone."

Nana's resultant smile let her know she'd said the right thing. "He was."

This was the first time anyone had ever opened up about her grandfather. She'd so many questions. "What did he do for a living?"

Her mother answered before her grandmother could. "He was an actuary in his nine-to-five job. On the weekends, he performed as a magician."

How cool was that? Leah looked at the picture again. It wasn't too hard to imagine him mesmerizing the audience with his dark good looks. "I bet he'd a rich, deep voice, somewhat accented, making him even more mysterious."

Her mother and Nana locked gazes, then turned in her direction. Her mother spoke first. "You're right."

Nana turned more slowly. Her eyes took on a slight sheen. "You have his gift. What else can you tell me?" She dabbed at her face with a cloth napkin.

Why was Nana asking her about a man she'd never met? Why would she know anything? She reached out for the picture, which her father placed in her hand. Thoughts poured into her head quickly, crowding against each other. Thoughts she'd have sworn had not been there before. She took on a thousand-yard stare as the thoughts gathered substance and became images in her mind.

Her grandfather was laying out the props for a magic show for a friend's birthday. They joked as they put a coffin on a sawhorse. Leah shared what her mind so vividly revealed. "He'd a close friend named Barney, who helped him set up for the show. His friend used to call him Ricky Ricardo because of his accent and his love of singing and dancing."

"Did you hear that, Adam? Maura?" Nana rotated her head, trying to catch each person's attention. Her fingers plucked a framed picture from the table. "Try this one. What do you get from it?"

Leah accepted the photo, turning it over to see that it was a wedding shot. A tide of passion and love hit her, almost knocking her off her feet.

She staggered a little bit, grabbed an empty chair, and slid into it. "Never did a man ever love a woman more than he did you."

Nana gave a little yelp. "That's what Buell always said. Leah has the gift. His gift was the secret of his shows. Most people didn't believe he could read minds and thought the people he brought up were shills. He didn't just read minds, he knew the people. I think that is what made him so likable."

"How is that?" Leah wouldn't have minded being likable.

Nana eyes glowed as she explained, almost as if lit by an internal source. "When he met someone, he knew what they needed to hear to be happy. He gave it to them. I scolded him once when he told an awkward fellow he would meet the girl of his dreams. My mistake was thinking no one would find the man attractive. Buell assured me there was such a woman, and after what he told him, the man would see her as the girl of his dreams. All he needed was a little encouragement."

"Dad really was magick in the best sense of the word," Leah's mother said. "He made our house the place to be. Kids wanted him to guess what they had in their hands or in their minds, which he did. They didn't freak the way adults did. Every day was a party, until he vanished." The jovial mood surrounding the table faded away, rather like the mythical Buell.

Nana caught Leah's hand and squeezed it. "Find him. Bring him back."

Really, how could she? She hadn't even mastered bringing herself back. Somehow, she was supposed to wander through time, pick the man up, and return him like an overdue library book. She opened her mouth to explain why such a task was impossible and noticed they were all staring at her. Their faces reflected varying degrees of optimism. It was easy to understand why Nana and Mother wanted her to bring Buell back, but her father looked just as hopeful. He could want to meet the man who'd inspired such stores. More likely, he just wanted his wife to be happy.

How would she have felt if someone had disappeared out of her life without an excuse or a goodbye? Truth was, she hadn't have liked it if Stella or even Dylan had left in the night. There would have been plenty of rumors, none of them true. She'd never know. Right now, she'd her fingers crossed she hadn't be the person who evaporated into thin air or shifted into another century. They were still staring at her, waiting for her answer. "Never fear, Nana. I will bring Grandfather back."

Why had she said that? Worse yet, they all wore identical expressions of relief, as if they thought she could. Did she need to remind them she was still a kid, a few months short of her seventeenth birthday, but still a kid? The best she'd managed in her lifetime was a science essay about how pigs weren't aerodynamically suited for flying. It had earned her third place in the science *Imagine* essay contest when she was in fifth grade. Truthfully, not too many kids had entered, which explained her third-place finish.

How did she all of a sudden become so powerful? Why did her family believe she could do the impossible? Ethan walked into the kitchen. He gazed at the adults, then at her, before asking, "Why are they all staring at you like that?"

"Oh, They're just expecting me to do the impossible." she muttered under her breath.

Ethan had a way of de-glorifying everything with a few words. All little brothers did, but he excelled at it. "Better get changed unless you want to shift in your nightshirt."

Leah took the opportunity to change, dashing from the kitchen to the open bathroom. For a few seconds, no one would expect anything miraculous from her. She pulled off her nightshirt quickly. So far, she'd appeared in the past in period clothing, but it would have been just her luck to show up in her Hello Kitty nightshirt or nothing at all. No time to waste while dressing, she removed the bandages from her legs, marveling at the smooth, unblemished skin. Nana's potion had worked. She looked at the back of her leg, where a jagged scar from her failure to become airborne from her flying attempt had existed. Nothing.

The bandages dropped to the floor as she examined the rest of her body. Lifting her arms up, she stretched up on her toes, then twisted one way, then the other. Nothing hurt, until she smacked the shower curtain rod. Their bathroom was not big enough for stretching out. The tub, stool, and sink crowded into a small space left a person barely enough room to turn around. Enough of that, she got dressed in her school clothes.

What if she time shifted today? Apparently, that's why her family had taken the day off. Had her mother called in and made her excuses? *Sorry, my daughter won't be in today. She's in another century changing the world for the betterment of all.* Did time pass the same in the other century? Did a day pass the same? Had it been a week or a year?

If she showed up with her skin smooth and healed, wouldn't it convince them she was a witch? Her plan of action would be not to show anyone her skin. When Miss Santiago talked about women coming a long way as far as rights and status, she'd no clue how far they had progressed from the Middle Ages.

Brushing her hair, she looked at herself in the mirror. With her long, dark hair and tattoo-free skin, nothing noticeably tied her to the twenty-first century. She'd read a novel once where a woman's smallpox scar had branded her a witch. No one her age had a smallpox scar, since smallpox no longer existed and there was no need for the vaccination.

Her pale skin definitely could use some help, though. Some foundation, blush, eyeliner, and mascara might help. She opened up her makeup bag and shook her bottle of moisturizer. Smoothing the lotion on her skin, she wondered about the advisability of makeup. How would her arch nemesis react to it? Sure, makeup had been around forever, but who had worn it? Was it the fast women, the evil folks, those guilty of a crime? Hard to know. It might be better just to be naked face.

Opening the door, she listened. A morning show blared from the living room while she could hear the clatter of dishes and running water in the kitchen. Someone was watching television, although she doubted it was her brother. Mother and Nana were cleaning the breakfast dishes. Her stomach growled, reminding her that she somehow had bypassed her last meal. That in itself wasn't too unusual. Breakfast usually consisted of what she could reasonably eat in the car.

It might do her well to eat breakfast, since she couldn't guarantee when she'd eat again. The memory of smoked, dried fish on her tongue sent her in search of cereal. Her father sat at the table poring over outdated encyclopedias, which meant her brother was watching the morning show with perky hosts and fluffy news that contributed nothing.

She sniffed the milk before pouring it on her cereal. It smelled okay today. She brought a spoon of cereal to her mouth and chewed. Stale, no big surprise there. When was the last time she'd eaten cereal? The only time her family ate breakfast together was when her father made pancakes on Sunday mornings. Weekends were her time to sleep in, even lately when she'd been helping her brother with his lawn moving endeavor. It wasn't too hard since most people didn't want to hear the sound of a lawnmower before ten in the morning.

Her father's eyes searched her face. She tried to ignore his staring. It was weird. For the most part, she mainly spoke to her family as they each hurried off to their job or school. All of a sudden, everyone watched her, just waiting for her to disappear. Instead of acknowledging his gaze, she read the nutrition facts printed on the cereal box. but that didn't stop his thoughts from coming at her.

Will this be the last time I ever see my baby girl? What kind of father have I been? Always working, staying late to finish projects, and even bringing work home. What type of childhood is that for her? She'll remember me as the father who was never there. Have I told her how wonderful she is? How proud I'm of her? How much I love her?

His thoughts were so strong they sounded like shouts in her mind. It was louder than Principal Sharpe's fears of Nana. "I know Dad, don't worry. You have always been and always will be a good father."

Her father's head snapped up. "You heard my thoughts?"

"Yes." She tilted her bowl to get the last of the milk.

"Damn," he swore under his breath.

Leah looked up. "I heard that."

Shaking his head, he said, "Wouldn't even matter. If I thought it, you'd still hear it."

"Maybe." She shrugged her shoulders. It was peculiar hearing her father's thoughts. Shouldn't some things be private? "It comes and goes. I found out Principal Sharpe is terrified of Nana."

Her father laughed, canted his chair back on two legs. "Any man with sense would be very afraid of your grandma. Not so much that she'd put the evil eye on him, but more that she can see into his soul and know who he really is, as opposed to the face he presents to the public."

It made her think of her grandmother in an entirely different way. "I'm not afraid of her. Neither are you."

"Not too much anymore. I used to be terrified of her," her father admitted with a sheepish grin.

Her analytical father wasn't in the habit of expressing a wide range of emotions. Just last night, she'd been traumatized her with the idea of the two of them being part of a wild, passionate love affair. It wasn't something she really liked to consider. Nana summed it up once by saying every generation thought they were the ones who'd created love and passion. This outlook made it hard to explain the existence of offspring. Leah shuddered at the thought. "Why did Nana scare you?"

Her father lowered his chair. His expression turned somber. "I figure she'd chase me away from your mother. I was the wrong type. One look into her shrewd face, and I knew she'd see I wasn't good enough for her daughter."

Leah pushed up against the table to stand and carried her dish to the sink. "None of that happened, so you had nothing to worry about."

Her father was silent, but his thoughts weren't. *Actually, all of it did happen, but Maura chose to fight for me.*

Leah did a double take at her father. Nope, his lips were not moving. Until he said, "You heard that too?"

That was hard to answer. It was like walking in on your parent when they were in the bathroom. You pretended it didn't happen so everyone could be comfortable. She bit her lip, stalling. What could she say? "Yes would embarrass him. No would be an obvious lie. She'd never mastered lying. Ah, yes, change the subject, "Do you think grandfather was a ceremonial magician?"

"I'm not sure. What I've heard about the ceremonial magicians is that they were very into details. Their rituals were precise and scientific in nature. Always done the right way at the right time. Might call them the engineers of the Wiccan world." Her father laughed at his joke, before continuing.

"They evolved from a type of priesthood. Some called them witches, but they always considered themselves better. It would be similar to someone comparing a chef to a cook. They both cook food, but the chef considers himself an artist." He stood and walked over to her, dusted her hair with a kiss. "As for you, I'll need to learn how to shield my thoughts."

"That's okay. I'll try not to listen. What am I going to do if I'm in a room with a whole bunch of people? Better yet, what if I hear someone say in his mind, 'I could kill him for that,' do I notify the police? People say that all the time when they're angry but don't really mean it." Goodness, this was supposed to help her out somehow. Already, it seemed like it had caused more trouble rather than providing any help. She rinsed her bowl and put it in the dishwasher. Her father stood with his mouth half open as he debated what he should say.

"It's okay if you don't know the answer. I don't know it, either," she reassured him.

He gave her a half salute and left the room. His last thought before leaving was about how his daughter reading his thoughts was like her seeing him in his underwear. Oh, Dad. How he'd ever fallen for her mom always amazed her. There had to have been other tightly laced students at college for him to associate with as opposed to her mother. It had to have been the lure of the forbidden. They'd initially met when her father had wandered into the Pagans United office as opposed to the Baptist Union next door. It had been her mother's turn to man the office, or woman the office, as she liked to put it.

If she didn't going to school today, what would she do? Sitting around wondering what might happen to her didn't appeal. She could get Nana to tell her more about her grandfather, maybe show her some more recent photos. Anything she'd would be at least twenty years old.

The house had a glassed-in porch the property owner called a Florida room. Nana liked it for growing the medicinal herbs she often used in medicine and rituals. The landlord, she remembered a man with a scraggly goatee, a receding hairline, and a ponytail. He could have been the poster boy for an aging hippie. She doubted he'd care what they grew as long as they paid the rent on time.

The smell of sandalwood incense met her before she walked into the room. Nana held a crystal in the stream of smoke, before placing it on the table and picking up a snowflake obsidian chunk. "What are you purifying the crystals for?"

"Your protection ritual," she said without turning around. "Your sister is here."

"What?" She hadn't heard Nora arrive. The choppy sound of a diesel engine car as it sputtered to a stop penetrated the walls. How did she do that? And why couldn't she read Nana's thoughts? Being able to tell where people were or when they were arriving might be a more useful skill to have.

Nora's throaty voice rumbled below her mother's and brother's voices. How her sister ended up sounding like some blues singer astounded her since she'd never smoked. She dashed to the living room. "Nora," she called out as she fell into her open arms. They both squeezed hard. Hard to believe she'd only been gone a few months.

Nora pulled back and looked at her thoroughly. Leah could hear her thoughts, not that she was trying to. They were there in her mind.

My little sister, she looks the same, but different. There's wariness about her that wasn't there before. I guess trying to stay alive, running from witch catchers, and being beaten half to death will do that to a person. What else has changed?

"I can hear your thoughts. That's another thing that has changed," she said, just in case her sister might go into some maudlin thought about this being the last time she'd see her little sister alive. She definitely could do without that. The doorbell rang, startling both of them.

Her mother answered the door, recognized the two women, and called them by name. One cotton-topped lady in a colorful wind suit and walking shoes reminded her of the quintessential grandmother. The woman spotted her and wrapped her in a talcum-scented hug.

"Oh, my dear, my dear, I came as soon as I heard."

Leah wondered if she was the talk of the Pagan community. If she remembered correctly, Helena, who was squeezing the daylights out of her, worked with animals. Somehow, Helena communed with them and eased their distress. She was a regular pet whisperer. It made Leah wonder what she'd do for her.

Zaharra, dressed in a colorful caftan complete with headscarf, was Nana's most serious competition. Nana called her faux Romany, declaring she didn't have a drop of gypsy blood, her ancestors were Swedes, and she dyed her hair. Yet, here she was. Her grandmother thanked her for coming. The woman gave Leah a measuring look.

I don't see anything special about the girl. This is all a big scam cooked up by Esmeralda Hare. I wouldn't put it past her.

Leah folded her arms, gave the woman a knowing look, and shook her head. The woman's false eyelashes fluttered, and then she acknowledged her. "Accept my apologies."

She angled her head to her grandmother. "I'm not the one you should be apologizing to."

Hurrying to Nana, the woman offered her apologies, begging forgiveness for any doubts. Her grandmother caught her eye and winked. Being able to hear thoughts wouldn't be a total waste after all. If she went to school today, maybe she'd hear Dylan's thoughts. She thought about who sat around her in geometry and how their thoughts would dribble over into her mind. Connor, who sat in front of her, drew naked women in his notebook. Did she want to hear his thoughts? No, there had to be a way to cut out people she didn't want to hear. She didn't hear Nana's thoughts.

That's because I don't want you to.

Leah looked at her grandmother, who smiled. Yes, Nana definitely had the skill. If only she could teach her. It also explained one reason why she was such a good fortune-teller. She knew the questions her clients didn't ask but wanted the answers to.

Four other older women came to the door. Her mother greeted them as Nana herded them to the backroom. Nora remarked near her ear, "It looks like all the old crones are here."

Her mother overheard them. "Yes, be grateful Nana knows so many. You two will be our only maidens. Some powerful magic will occur here today. Speaking of that, Nana ordered me to prepare you with bathing."

Leah pretended to sniff her pits. "Do I smell?"

Nora put her arm around her shoulder. "I'll talk to you while you soak."

Their mother held up her hand. "Nora can start the bath, sprinkle the herbs, even bless you, but the bath time should be used for contemplation and purification."

"Yes, Mother," they said in unison.

Leah understood the dynamics of rituals. It was like going to church and never listening to the sermon, contemplating the stained-glass windows or bemoaning the lack of cute boys instead of listening, and then one day realizing the sermon was about you. Yep, that's where she was. The ritual was about her.

Chapter Ten

THE WATER SLOWLY filled the tub for the ceremonial bath as Nora pawed through a her box filled with colorful silk bags. "I see we still have the same sucky water pressure."

Leah nodded. Of course, as Pagans they never complained about water pressure, never thought they could. People assumed they could put a hex on someone to get them to do as they wanted, or just threaten and that would be it. The law of three would bite them in the butt if they ever thought about doing it. It was similar to the golden rule, only three times as bad. Whatever you did would come back to you threefold. If you were nice to other people, then other people would be nice to you.

Nora opened a bag, sprinkling some in the water. "Angelica, for protection against negative energy, and it draws positive energy to your side."

Leah quipped, "I can definitely use that."

Her sister held up four bags and waited for her attention. The bath itself was part of the ritual. Nora had changed. They used to joke about being the kids of a witch, but her sister acted as if she took it seriously. It could have been because her little sister's life was on the line. In that case, it was all good.

"Sister mine, these four are for protection: arnica, basil, bay leaf, and blessed thistle. The thistle is especially potent and should aid you, being a medieval herb." The herbs floated through the air before coming to a rest on the water. Once in the water, they steeped, perfuming the air with a rich, earthy aroma that reminded her of the various herbs shops Nana insisted on dragging her through when she needed extra ingredients. She always liked the smell of the shops.

Opening another bag, Nora took a large handful and released it into the flowing water. "Balsam fir for strength. I gave you extra because I figured you needed it."

"Thank you." She did need all the strength and cunning she could get. A troop of well-armed soldiers wouldn't hurt, either. She inhaled the steam filling the room. "It smells like an evergreen tree."

"It does," Nora agreed. "I'm going to ruin all these great smells by adding camphor."

Camphor? Leah's nose wrinkled. Camphor is what they used to keep the moths away from their winter clothes. Unlike cedar, it didn't smell good. "Why?"

"Camphor increases your psychic divination. If you know what you're walking into, then you can develop solutions. That, along with your ability to read people's thoughts, should stand you in good stead." She dropped a small white block into the water.

The smell of mothballs filled the room, making her cough. "I'm not sure I can stand that."

Her sister gave her a sympathetic smile. "You will." Nora lit the white votive candles on the rim of the tub and the toilet back. With each candle, she called on a different entity. "Artemis, give my sister strength." She touched the lit match to the biggest candles. "Isis, guard my sister." All the candles glowed gently, casting a golden light over the crowded bathroom, masking some of its untidiness.

Pulling a bottle out of her pants pocket, her sister placed it on the sink corner. "Sandalwood oil. Make sure you anoint yourself with it when you're finished. It will help seal in the magick. Don't forget to scrub down with the salt first." The bathroom door closed softly behind

Nora.

Too bad she couldn't have stayed. It would have been good to talk to someone about everything that was happening in her life. For reasons unknown, Mom chose to talk about how crazy in love she and Dad were, and still are. Then she found out her never-talked-about grandfather was a likable fellow who may or may not have been a ceremonial magician. He also might not be dead, but possibly fallen through time. If she could pick him up on her way back from dark and scary times that would be nice.

As if.

If she could figure out a way to stop going back, she'd. The various herbs' smells mingled, but the camphor dominated. Dropping her clothes, she reached for the salt paste and rubbed the rough mixture all over her body, avoiding her eyes. Not only would it flake off bad energy, but it would do a number on dead skin cells, too. Her skin would be glowing and protected. *Think of it not as a protection ritual to chase the bogeyman away, but as a spa day,* Leah told herself as she climbed into the tub. The water was hot, but not hot enough to burn her.

Her father used to joke that their landlord was smart because he made sure the temperature on the water heater was set low enough that none of them could ever level a lawsuit against him for burning themselves. Leah placed one foot in the water, then the other and gently lowered her body into the steamy broth. It was as if she were part of a stew, the main ingredient.

Leaning back against the tub, she closed her eyes. For a brief second, she worried about shifting in the nude, but she felt safe and protected in the water. Whatever power was in the herbs enveloped her. It probably didn't hurt to have thirteen witches in the house. Since the majority of them were about Nana's age, it meant they'd have plenty of experience.

How had she called her spirit guide? It had been so long. Something about a beach, she remembered that much. The image of a beach with gentle waves took form in her mind. Seagulls called to one another. The clouds bunched together, filtering most of the sun, but the air was still warm and humid. As she walked, the sand shifted under her bare feet, and the air carried the tang of fish. She tried to make her mind as blank as possible as she observed the scenery around her and simply existed. Suddenly, she was no longer alone. Two beings stood on either side of her. What was this?

"No worries, friend," her guide assured her.

Ah, yes, it was Jamaican Man, as she'd dubbed her guide in earlier times when they'd seen each other. He'd once told her his name was Lowe, which she thought was a peculiar name.

"Why are there two of you?" She was unwilling to look to her left at the unknown presence. It didn't feel hostile. Far from it, she felt warmth, acceptance, and some amusement.

"Sometimes you need more than one. The guides come, as needed. Look at your new friend."

Turning her head slightly, she took in the form of a woman about her height. A sense of familiarity overwhelmed her. It was Nana at a younger age. The features were so familiar. Didn't she see the same ones in the mirror every day? "Are you an earlier version of my grandmother?"

The woman smiled at her. "No, I'm an older version of you. Take heart, Leah, you will make it through this trial, wiser and stronger."

The thought did cheer her some, but spirit guides were often a facet of yourself you reached through meditation. This wasn't an actual older her, which meant she could still die or get stuck in the past.

Lowe clucked his tongue. "Don't be going there, girl. You know as well as I we act as we think. If you think bad thoughts, you'll have bad results. You're a champion. If I was a betting man and you were a horse, I would place my money on you."

Leah imagined herself being a horse in a race, stretching her long neck forward to win by a nose. "Thanks. I will win this race. What do I need to know?"

Her future self spoke. "Number one, things are not as they seem. People might say they do something for one reason, but they don't. Often, the reason is so deep, even They're clueless."

Leah spoke more to herself than her guides. "My ability to read thoughts would be of no help."

Lowe landed a hearty pat on her back that caused her to stumble a little. "What did I tell you, little bird? No bad thoughts. Know this. People do everything out of greed or fear. In the dark times, mostly fear. Fear of not being able to survive, fear of being snatched up as a witch, fear of not being loved, let them go. It was a dark time, not much love going around. Even greed was another way to stockpile against fear. Gold will buy food, protection, or even company to keep the fear at bay. Remember this."

It made sense. She usually reacted out of fear, not greed. She wanted to ask some more questions, but Lowe shimmered and faded. Quickly turning, she discovered that her future self had blinked out of existence, too. She was all alone on the beach. Even the gulls had disappeared into the clouds, and a long, ominous roll of thunder sounded as the sky darkened.

A loud hammering dissolved the beach scene. "Leah, are you awake?" Her mother's voice carried a sense of urgency. The woman would barrel into the bathroom if she didn't answer, pull her dripping body out of the tub, and start CPR. Locks were another thing their property owner wasn't big on. It must be disappointing to her mother to have gotten all this medical training and not be able to use it on her family.

"I'm okay." Stepping out of the tub, she reached for the towel Nora had left behind. She held the unfamiliar towel up and sniffed it. It was new. Hard to miss the symbolism: unused towel for the virgin. She refused to be a sacrifice.

Mother's voice carried clearly into the room. "It's time. Wear the robe Nora left for you."

A quick glance revealed the door not entirely shut. A flowing robe of blues and greens with a touch of silver hung on the back of the door. Nora must have put it there when Leah had been conversing with her guides. She'd certainly have remembered such an elegant garment.

"Just the robe," her mother instructed.

"Got it." First the oil, then the robe. She glanced back at the still-flickering candles. Ideally, she should put them out. Blowing them out would scatter her luck, and she didn't need that. Instead, she made a mental note to send her brother to take care of them.

Her hands smoothed the sandalwood oil down her arms in slow strokes, she thought of all it represented. Nana called it the workhorse of the oils because it aided in spirituality, protection, meditation, and healing. All good things she could use. Her hand stilled as she rubbed it against her belly, realizing it was also a component in spells to induce lust or love. "Not today."

The last thing she needed was for Lionel to remember his childhood crush on her. Nope. She didn't need some medieval lurker to complicate her life even more. Rubbing the oil into her elbows, she wondered, *Would it be so bad if he loved me? Don't you treat people nice if you love them?*

A memory of a recent court case of a woman who'd killed in the name of love played havoc with her theory. Still, had Lionel ever loved her? It was hard to decide what constituted love back in the olden days. The man obviously felt some ownership or rights over her. When she'd moved on, he'd felt the need to punish her, and obviously those who bore any similarity to her. It described more of a psychotic obsession as opposed to love.

As she pulled the robe off the hook, a tingling passed through her fingers. No doubt, as she'd bathed, the robe had undergone numerous blessings. If she'd been in a cartoon, a glow would have emanated from the robe. She felt a tangible presence pulsating inches from the fabric. She slipped on the garment, and it rested in the air instead of against her body. Enchantments lay warm and thick against her skin.

Leah pulled the hair tie loose and ran a brush through her hair. Always best to put your best face forward for the Lord and Lady, her mother would always say. Her grandmother had become a solid Goddess worshipper and had left the Lord behind, probably due to Grandfather's disappearance. Knowing Nana, it was her form of protest.

The face in the mirror reminded her of her older self, but that woman had seemed at peace. Leah envied her. She'd known what she was about and who she was. Then again, she'd already conquered her greatest trial.

Even though it was day, the house was dark, every curtain, every blind pulled shut against the light and possibly curious neighbors. They weren't party throwers, so the series of cars decorated with bumper stickers announcing *Friend of the Fae, Something Wiccan This Way Comes,* and *My Other Vehicle Is a Broom* were bound to attract some attention. The smell of incense and burnt matches wafted toward her. She could hear chanting in the distance.

Her mother waited in the hall with the ceremonial hood of her robe up. Her motionless stance allowed her to blend into the shadows. Leah startled a little when her mother placed a hand on her.

"Come, I will bring you in. The circle has been cast and the ritual started," her mother said in an authoritarian voice, which she never used at home.

Leah stifled her offhand reply and answered instead with, "I'm ready."

Her father stood at the doorway arch of the room and announced, "The maiden approaches."

A flurry of rattling sounds and furious drumming greeted his announcement. Leah knew the group was women only. Allowing her father to participate to such a small extent was a huge concession. Thank the Goddess, because she could use all the good energy she could get.

The chanting resumed, gaining energy with her approach, but she felt a tugging. Her gaze flickered downward. Her mother's hand was no longer touching hers, but the feeling of tugging increased. Her mother sketched an opening in the circle wall. Leah walked through, and the tugging stopped. It was like walking into a sauna of energy, thick, warm, and heavy as it surrounded her on every side. The women turned and touched her, urging her toward the end of the table, where Nana's important occasions white-lace tablecloth covered the rolling desk chair. Leah carefully took her seat, very aware of how the chair could get away from her at inopportune moments. The chair and she did not seem to get along.

Tucking her fingers under the edge of the chair, she held on, least it surprise her once again. One woman called for order, stilling the music. Nana stood, holding her palms up and out. She nodded her head in Leah's direction. "Thank you, maidens, mothers, and sister crones for coming to the aid of my granddaughter. You're all powerful forces to be reckoned with on your own, but united with the Goddess, the force of Mother Earth, the Elements, and the combined forces of honor, compassion, and love, none can prevail." Nana's voice gathered power and majesty as she spoke, ending in a crescendo that would have made many a wizard proud.

The women reached for one another's hands, creating another circle within the original circle. Leah held out her hands, only to have them clasped by her sister and her mother. When had they ended up on either side of her? They must have followed her in. It was reassuring to have them on either side. Nana walked behind her and interwove her fingers in Leah's hair.

The chanting started at the far end of the table and caught as if it were a wildfire burning toward her. "Oh, Great Goddess, Creator of All, watch over your creation. Protect Leah from all harm, evil intent, and those set upon harming her. Open her eyes, so she can see the hearts and intentions of those around her."

Leah closed her eyelids to better concentrate on the spell. The words were similar to what her spirit guide had said. People's words often hid their intentions. Could Henry mean her harm and Lionel want to save her? It made no sense. By the end of the ritual, things would become clearer. The heat, incense, and energy lulled her into a meditative state. Her spirit drifted high in the corner, looking down at everyone. A group of women held hands tightly as if playing a very competitive game of Red Rover. They chanted, some swayed, and a few had their eyes closed as she did, while others looked upward, fixed on other realms.

From the corner of the room, she saw her bent head with Nana standing behind her, her hands resting on her hair. Her grandmother had her head thrown back, calling out in a language she assumed to be Romany because she could not understand it.

Her older self appeared and held out her hand, mouthing the word, "Come." She looked back at the group, wondering if she should leave her own ceremony.

Her other self whispered, "This is your vision. You must know it to succeed."

It made sense in a way that strange things she'd never done before made sense. Reaching out, she grasped her older self's hand. In a twinkling, they disappeared only to reappear in a damp, stone room smelling of mold. Two priests sat at a trestle table.

The younger priest looked up, revealing the young Lionel's curling locks and deep-set eyes. "Abbot, I realize it is an honor to be a servant of Christ, but is it also not an honor to be a husband who sires children? Making even more to follow Christ?"

The older man pushed back his hood, revealing a tonsured head. "It is good you give this much thought before taking your final vows. There are many who are able to be father and husband. There are few who are capable of joining the exclusive brotherhood of clergy."

Her older self hissed, "Expensive," when the man said *exclusive*. Leah made a mental note to ask her later what she'd meant.

Lionel bobbed his head, agreeing with the older man. "It's a special privilege to be part of the Church, but I believe my place is to walk the ordinary path. I've a girl waiting for me. We have pledged our troth to one another."

The sincerity shining from Lionel's face stirred Leah's heart. He really did love her.

The abbot stood in a hurry, knocking back his stool. "A girl. Fie on her. You have not defiled yourself with her?"

"No, Father," Lionel answered, eyes downcast, while color mounted his cheeks.

Even though Arabella knew he'd never taken liberties with her, it appeared that her medieval lover had strayed from the chaste path. She wondered how she'd feel about this as a woman of that period. Would she expect as much? How would she feel if Dylan confessed to sleeping with Alexis or Lauren? That would be a bit much to accept. It was better not to know. She could not hold anything he'd done before he'd met her against him now. Maybe that was how Arabella felt.

Lionel found his cuticles intriguing as the old man placed a bowl on the table. The abbot poured water from an oaken bucket into a silver bowl. He moved his hands over it several times, allowing some powder to slip from his fingers into the water. The water bubbled once, then became opaque.

Leah whispered to her guide, "What's he doing?"

Her guide whispered back, "The old toad is up to no good. He's using charlatan tricks to fool the earnest lover."

Lionel's head went up to stare at the priest. "Divination is not allowed."

The priest waved his hand as if to shoo away the words. "Divination is not allowed because many cannot control it as I can. Rest assured what you're about to see is best for you."

"Notice he didn't say true," her guide mentioned.

Leah shifted her position behind the priest to see more.

Shapes slithered across the water as the priest questioned Lionel. "Tell me about this girl you love."

Lionel's face took on a dreamy expression. "She's beautiful."

An image of a blonde maiden with blue eyes shimmered in the water. Leah knew that couldn't be her and wondered what game the priest played.

Lionel continued to talk, not looking at the water, "Her hair is dark, as are her eyes."

The priest held his hands over the water, and the image changed as if the old man willed it. Leah could see between his outspread fingers. It looked like her in a vague way that the woman was female with dark hair. "Tell me more," the abbot urged.

Lionel sighed a little, reflecting on his love. "She has a strong chin and straight white teeth and a smallish nose. Dark, winged brows frame her eyes." The image changed as Lionel described her. Leah hated to admit it, but it looked more and more like her.

Smiling a little to himself, the man held his large hands over the bowl. "How long since you've seen the wench?" He coughed, then said, "I meant, girl."

"Two years now." Lionel looked thoughtful. "Soon, she'll be thirteen summers, old enough to wed and bed. She is especially fond of colors and

glittery objects, rather like a magpie," he added with a chuckle.

Thirteen was old enough to wed. The sixteen-year-old version of herself hadn't actually had a real date yet. The man made a few more moves with his hand, dressing the water version in red and turning her sideways, probably to prevent Lionel from recognizing it wasn't her. A man materialized beside her in fine court clothes and a pointed beard. He began to kiss and caress her as Arabella responded to his caresses as lustily as any porn star.

"Look! Look at your beloved and how she comports herself in your absence," the man yelled, pointing to the water.

Lionel looked with avid interest, his brow furrowed, and he bit his bottom lip. "She never lets me kiss her on the lips. Why would she act in such a manner? Who is this man?"

The abbot picked up the bowl containing the writhing couple and poured the water back into the bucket. "The man makes no matter. The important thing is the woman played you false. Women are not to be trusted. Her love for you was turned aside, all for a bag of colorful material."

Leah looked at her guide in horror. "I became a slut for fabric? I think not."

"Remember," her guide pressed her hand against her arm, "things are not as they seem. That devious man is able to extract people's thoughts and use them to create his illusions. Lionel saw you because he wanted to believe."

"He wanted to believe Arabella could be unfaithful to him. The girl is barely a teenager," Leah complained, irritated that she could do no more than float about in an ethereal fashion. She was so angry she'd prefer to stride with purpose, kick something or, better yet, someone.

"Twelve is old enough to marry," her guide reminded. "It is also obvious to Lionel that he won't be going back to you. The church expects noble families to contribute generously to the church coffers when one of their own is behind the walls. Lionel cannot follow his heart. He knows this on some level. To deal with this knowledge, he already believes you will play him *false. It doesn't mean it will hurt any less. In your relationship, he was the one who always loved more."*

"Still." Leah felt the need to defend Arabella, but her guide pointed to the drama unfolding before them.

Lionel clutched his chest as if he'd taken a direct hit. "Why would she deny me for a dress?"

The abbot shook his head. "Such is the way of women. Their nature is low and base. God has placed man below the angels, while woman is below the animals. A faithful steed, hound, or an ox can be better trusted than a female."

Below the animals? Now, that might have been true for some girls she could name, but not her. She narrowed her eyes at the man talking gibberish, fisted her hands on her hips, as she glared at the old fool. Apparently, he couldn't feel her look. He continued to fill Lionel's ears with nonsense.

"Good thing you came into the service of our Lord before you were misled by the lies that fall from honeyed lips. Women cause men to stray from the good way as Eve deceived Adam."

Worse yet, Lionel nodded, agreeing with his statements. Of course, at that time, it was what people believed. She found it hard to believe that the pretty Arabella, who'd refused to let Lionel kiss her, had thrown up her skirts at the first man who'd come her way. She'd no doubt Arabella's family pressured her to choose elsewhere, but part of her still cared for Lionel.

"Women are the devil." The man's voice vibrated with hate. "They have intercourse with Satan! and hand over their souls to him. Know this now."

Lionel cradled his head in his hands, and his shoulders shook as he wept. Leah watched in surprise.

The abbot frowned at the display of emotion and turned promptly toward the cupboard. Uncorking a decanter, he poured some wine into a wooden goblet. Using his body to block his actions, he shook powder into the cup and stirred it with his finger.

The guide pointed to the cup. "Here it starts. He gets the young priests hooked on a potion he's concocted. They become dependent on him for their supply, willing to do whatever he tells them."

What he'd put in the cup also explained the skeletal, drugged look of the Lionel she'd seen before. "I thought drugs weren't really popular until later."

The older Leah sniffed. "Reading the history books again. The Crusaders brought many types of drugs back with them. Wily men like Abbot Augustus there knew enough to demand a steady supply. He also had a ready supply of guinea pigs to try his potions on. Ever wonder how soldiers managed to kill infidel women and children without their actions sickening them? The drugged wine they consumed before slaughtering innocents could either wipe their minds of the memories or cause the fleeing children to appear to be monsters. It wouldn't be the first time soldiers went into battle with drug-fogged brains. Watch Lionel to see what symptoms he displays."

The abbot handed the cup to Lionel. "Drink all of it, son. It will help you forget the faithless wench."

Her guide pressed her fingers into Leah's arms, returning them back to the Florida room filled with stoked women whose chants sounded tired and forced. The ritual was coming to an end, which made it the perfect time to return to her body.

CHAPTER ELEVEN

THE WOMEN BEGAN to sing a song about the circle being open but unbroken. Leah sensed this without seeing it, just as she knew her father had stepped into the room now that the ritual had ended. No one would complain about his masculine energy as if it were a contaminant. Her mother still grasped one hand, while Nora wove her fingers through hers. Nana left her position at her back to herd her fellow witches into the kitchen.

Savory smells wafted from the kitchen as the women opened up or heated dishes they'd brought. Nana rounded up close to every plate they owned amid the clatter of dishes and silverware. Their family was not in the habit of serving more than six, which may have been all the plates they had.

Mother's grip tightened and loosened as she stood. "I should go help."

Nora kept a silent vigil with her in companionable silence. In some ways, Leah was rather like Helen Keller. Adrift in a world none of them knew or could understand. Her eyelids stayed closed as she allowed her mind to examine the revelations she'd received.

The older her seemed to have a deeper knowledge of the myriad things that motivated the human heart. The abbott's motivation puzzled her. Did he truly think women were the source of evil? Sure, there were chauvinistic males now who thought men were superior to women, but that was the extent of it. They might keep mental lists of jobs not suitable for a female. Sometimes they might express their opinions loudly. Overall, though, they posed no danger to her or the way of life of most American women.

The abbot needed to punish women as much as he needed to enslave the young priests. His potion should do the trick. She'd heard about soldiers in various wars becoming morphine addicts. The abbot might just be doing what those in power had done before him and after. Lionel used to be such a sweet, idealistic individual. Leah realized she felt compassion for the boy he used to be. The crazed, angry priest Lionel had evolved into did not merit her sympathy.

Someone in the kitchen called Nora's name, causing her to let go of Leah's hand. Her sister kissed her hair in passing and whispered, "Be safe, little sister."

That's all it took. With Nora leaving and letting go of her hand, the tugging increased, reminiscent of some horror movie she'd watched where tiny people lived under the floorboards. They were not kind, helpful brownies. No, these people were cruel and devious. It felt like they were pulling on her from all sides. She struggled to release the pull of the past. Maybe seeing Nana's plants scattered around the room would help break her trance.

Her eyelids popped open at about the same time that she sank deeper into the chair, dropping into another dimension. Nora's voice echoed as she fell: "Leah's fading. Stop her."

She fell, aware she was passing through time, seeing flashes of color and light. That had never happened before. What was different? Instead of hitting the ground in a clumsy heap, she floated to the ground rather like Mary Poppins, but with no umbrella.

She gently touched the ground with her bare feet settling on the cold-packed dirt. Tall trees threw out intimidating shadows with the setting sun.

Once she made full contact with the ground, she shook out her robe. Her hands bunched the wide skirt of the voluminous blue and green robe. She still had it on. That was odd.

From behind the trees appeared a few heads. In the fading light, she thought she made out the features of Henry and Sabina. Henry eased around the tree, checking out her dress in detail. "Your garment is passing strange for these parts."

Sabina, possibly emboldened by Henry's behavior, stepped out from the tree with a swagger, as if she weren't afraid. "You fell out of the heavens like an angel, a fallen angel." Sliding closer, she reached out to touch the richly decorated fabric.

The instant Sabina's fingers touched the cloth, she yelped. "The fabric burned me. It isenchanted. You're a witch."

Ideally, she knew the robe was supposed to help her. Although all it seemed to be doing now was confirming her witch status. Still, she wondered if that was the plan. Instead of cowering and awaiting death, she was to stand strong. Now would be a good time to start as any. "I'm a witch. The gown is enchanted."

Old Margaret stepped out from behind a tree, pointing a gnarled finger at her. "You bear the blame for my house gone."

"Not really." Leah held her hands out in front of her as if she could stop the words and the incipient guilt they carried. "Ignorance and fear are the culprits, not me."

Turning in Henry's direction, she asked, "Didn't you tell me your property was seized for the church after the mayor named you a witch?"

"This is true," he agreed, and then placed a small twig between his teeth to chew. His brow furrowed in thought. Pulling the stick out of his mouth, he gestured with it. "The mayor had need to put me out of the way. Once I confronted him with the knowledge I knew he be cheating the townsfolk by only giving them back a percentage of the grain they brought in to be milled.

Enough angry villagers would have turned on him as opposed to me, Old Margaret, or Sabina."

Leah listened, familiar with Henry's tale, but she wanted the others to hear it again. Strange how someone else they knew repeating the same premise that she wasn't to blame sounded more believable from lips other than hers. "In my time, they'd refer to Margaret and Sabina as collateral damage. They didn't do anything wrong, but just to have Henry, a man, accused as a witch would appear suspicious, especially if it were known he'd disagreed with the mayor."

Taking a cautious step forward, Margaret slowly circled Leah. Fearing the woman wasn't in her right mind after the destruction of her home and the loss of her beloved cat, Leah turned with her, never allowing the woman behind her back. The woman might have been packing a sharp knife.

Sabina placed both hands on her hips and gave Henry a knowing look. "People knew there was bad blood between Henry and the mayor. The village wanted Henry to be the mayor because he was a fair man, but the title is an appointed one. Rumors were that money changed hands to ensure the title fell as it did."

"Not rumors, 'tis the truth," Henry said, the anger in his face gathering like storm clouds. "All the more reason to be rid of me." Kicking at a rock in the path with his booted foot, he swore something indistinct, most likely directed at the mayor.

In some ways, Henry was the natural leader of the villagers. It paid to get rid of your strongest competition first. How convenient the church just happened to have these witch trials to help remove the troublesome element. "Why do you think there are all these accusations flying about cattle dying, crops failing, and witches? It is obvious the mayor uses it to get rid of people he doesn't like, but why does it work?"

Old Margaret answered first. "Times have always been tough. The earth makes us work hard to bring forth food. Calves, lambs, and even children die often before birth. Our sin causes bad things to happen, but no one wants to be guilty of causing their own child to die, so it is easier to blame someone else."

The urge to correct the old woman about the true nature of sin died a quick death. These people only knew what the priests had told them. Their minds were not exactly receptive vessels waiting for her to pour knowledge into them. "Still, like you said, Margaret, people have had problems all through the centuries. Why start blaming witches? What does it mean to be a witch?"

Sabina cocked her head curiously. "You call yourself a witch. Mayhap you should tell us?"

"True," Leah agreed, realizing it was the first time she'd ever called herself a witch in public. She'd gone to the regional meetings where people assumed she must be a witch because of her mother and grandmother, but still that hadn't always rung true. It had to be a personal experience. You weren't a witch due to your relatives. "My kind of witch is not what you think. I'm bound to work for the good of all and the harm of none. I honor both people and nature. Many Wiccans in my time choose not to eat meat, to honor their fellow creatures."

Henry shook his head as if astounded. "That is more than passing strange." Interlacing his fingers, he turned out his palms and cracked his knuckles. "I've given much thought to all that you have said. I've thought on it before. Those of us who cannot read are at a disadvantage. The clergy say the Bible tells us to do this witch killing, but we cannot read to see if it is so. Scripture translation suits whoever is in power. Heard tell in France and Italy, the clerics meet to vote on which Scriptures they will believe. King James, a powerful man afraid of witches, put out the edict for the last rewriting."

"The man is trying to deny his destiny." Margaret cackled. "Rumor was a fortune-teller told him a witch would cause his death. Seems fitting that he rid himself of all."

Sabina strutted in a circle until she gained everyone's attention. "A visiting tinker I happened to strike up an acquaintanceship with had been up to London. He told me all about the king."

Margaret gazed at Henry and Leah. "That explains the new pots you acquired."

Sticking her nose in the air and ignoring the old woman's remarks, Sabina continued. "King James' favorites are all men, three especial men."

Henry and Margaret gasped in response, but Leah couldn't figure out what was special about having friends. Didn't kings have friends? Then it hit her. Special friends. But that wasn't okay in these times. "Aren't there laws against having special friends if you're a man, and those friends are men?"

"Yes," Sabina answered, smacking her fist into her hand. "Kings don't follow laws like we do. Who will punish them?"

She'd a point. "Do you think this whole witch hunt is a smoke screen to keep people from finding out about his boyfriends?"

Henry stroked his chin. "I hope not. I imagine that, besides his wife, most folks do not care what James does. It has been the way of kings to blame others. There's also word of Jews, lepers, and gypsies bringing plagues and pestilence. Then again, most people do what benefits them the most. Right now, chasing us out of town benefits them. I do not believe they even want us to go to trial. It is best that we vanish. If we went to trial, I would say all I know, causing questions to grow in the minds of fellow villagers."

Leah understood what Henry was proposing. "You're saying we should just pick up and go elsewhere? What about your property?"

"It is the best solution. I believe my townspeople do not want to put me to the test and have me die in the testing. When I saw which way the wind blows, my cousin and I traveled to the next village to have a deed drawn up that transfers my land to my cousin. My land stays in my family, instead of going to the church. If the mayor moves against my cousin, then he'll do it with scrutiny, because all will remember how he was with me. I do not think the move too difficult." Henry shrugged his shoulders as if it were nothing.

The man had to be one of the most easygoing she'd ever run across. He reminded her of her father in some ways. Margaret didn't share his attitude. She stomped her feet, ignoring the pain that must have been resonating through her bare feet. "Easy for you, Henry. Your cousin has pledged to take care of you. In one fell swoop, he has all he ever wanted. I've nothing. Nothing, do you hear me? What little I had burned to the ground." Her eyes cut to Leah, letting her know she still blamed her.

Henry strode to the trembling woman and wrapped an arm around her shoulders. "I will take care of you. I feel beholden since my initial charge may have compounded the accusations leveled against you and Sabina."

Sabina folded her arms and tapped her toe, as if waiting for Henry to say something. She cleared her throat when that didn't work. Henry let go of Margaret and threw up his hands.

"I suppose you want me to offer to care for you, too." Henry said the words as if put upon. Sabina smiled, looking up through her lashes, in an expression that may have garnered her more than new pots. "I'm not sure what good it would do either of us. A new town will be full of new prospects for you. They won't approach you if they think you're under my care. On the other hand, I doubt I want to go to the trouble to look after you to have you take off when someone more to your taste arrives."

Sabina bit her lips, and then concurred. "You're right. You can be my brother wherever we stop."

Leah watched all this interaction and wondered what it meant for her. She wasn't here to be part of a traveling band of misfit would-be witches. Still, until the universe made her path a little clearer, she'd follow along. The sunlight streaming through the leaves reminded her it was daytime. The breeze chilled her slightly, making her wonder what month it was. Both

Margaret and Sabina sported shawls, although Sabina wore hers wrapped around her hips, cinching her skirt closer, no doubt to emphasize her curves. Margaret huddled under hers, shivering as if she'd never be warm again.

Henry, on the other hand, wore a loose tunic-like shirt and a rough vest over it. He didn't act cold. Leah was sure men somehow stayed warmer in archaic times, unless it was uncool for a guy to act cold. In the mornings when her father drove her to school, there were plenty of jacketless boys at the bus stop, who acted as if they didn't have a care in the world. Some of them did look a little on the frozen side.

If things went well, somehow she'd bump into Grandpa, recognize him despite the twenty-year gap since his last picture, grab him, and return home. It sounded like a good plan to her, with only a few possibilities of going very wrong. She hadn't find Grandpa. There was also the chance he liked it just fine here, which could be the real reason he'd never come back. Nope, she did not want to tell Nana that. Some people might think her grandmother was already in the angry mode, but currently she just lingered in the strong-willed and opinionated department. Leah never wanted to see her move up to angry.

There was her mission, as well, or the mission her family thought she was on. Was it a heroic mission like Joan of Arc's? She doubted it. Was it a personal mission, more like solving something in her past so she could return to her present? If so, what did she have to do? Lionel figured into it somehow, but that was the limit to her insight. That, and someone she trusted would betray her. Her eyes drifted to the three figures in front of her.

Sabina danced beside Henry, taking every opportunity to touch his arm and point out something. Leah's lips twisted as she thought Henry mentioned a wife and family. That made no matter to Sabina. She was an opportunist. Nana would call her a gold digger. It must be natural for her to latch on to whatever man was around. The woman would definitely throw her under the bus, or in this case the wagon, if it would benefit her somehow.

Then there was Margaret. The woman leaned heavily on the walking stick Henry had cut for her. She'd no qualms of letting Leah know she blamed her for everything, from the destruction of her house and livelihood to the disappearance of her feline. Margaret might not mean to harm her, but her loud protests would be enough to convict her.

Henry's back was straight, his head held high, as he moved easily through the woods. Compared to the other villagers, the man obviously ate well and was in excellent health. His robust appearance varied greatly from the villagers with their frail frames, sunken cheeks, and lackluster expressions. Why was Henry in such good health?

July was the starving month. She remembered that from history class. People butchered their livestock in the winter. All through the winter months, they ate well on the harvest and meat. Spring was the time of sowing. By July, often their supplies ran out and nothing was ready to harvest. People often resorted to eating grass and anything else vaguely edible.

It was summer here. The canopy of trees was full and thick, not like the new growth of spring. Even though it seemed chilly, she reminded herself that seventy degrees was sometimes as high as it got for a British summer in the twentieth century. Added to that, they were in a shadowy woods and five hundred years in the past. It made sense it could be summer. With that in mind, Leah's eyes rested on Henry. Of course, he'd be in good spirits if anticipating a generous reward for walking in trusting witches.

As preposterous as the thought seemed, she knew she was right. Her spirit guide had emphasized it would be someone she trusted. It was hard to betray someone who didn't trust you, simply because such actions were expected. Should she find out Henry's motives? Her pace slowed more as she contemplated her actions. If she got close enough to Henry, she might be able to scan his thoughts. So far, that little talent had turned out to be inconsistent, not working when she needed it and only working with people whose thoughts she pretty much knew already.

If she could get close enough, she'd read Henry's thoughts to decide what his true intentions were. The sun broke through the canopy, highlighting the trio in front of her. She stopped, looking at the three of them as they came to a standstill. The sunlight bounced off something shiny. Flashes of silver peeked through the greenery. Leah didn't need to be told it was a trap.

Slipping silently off the path, she searched for a climbable tree. Her best prospect's lowest limb loomed just out of reach. The women's screams echoed through the forest. She quickly pulled herself up into the tree. Climbing higher, she tried to ignore the shouts. The robe made it surprisingly easy to scamper up the tree, clinging close to her body instead of catching on limbs. The blue-green coloring disguised her among the leaves as well.

Crouched on a limb, she tried to slow her breathing. They might be able to find her just by listening for her panicky breathing. She reminded herself to inhale slowly through her nose. Her legs were starting to hurt from her crouched position. Definitely not a bird in another life. Her perch felt unsure, as if any type of movement might end with her falling to the ground. A rustling of leaves alarmed her. Turning her head slightly, she found herself almost within kissing distance of a brown snake that seemed equally surprised to see her.

Great, she was probably in its tree. Were snakes like dogs? If she didn't show fear, would it leave her alone? The sounds of masculine voices and horses alerted her to men right below. The large draft horses carrying armored knights trampled the undergrowth, sending a variety of forest inhabitants scurrying for safety. Leah made the mistake of looking away from the snake to observe what was happening below.

Henry, mounted on a horse, pointed in the direction they'd come. "She was right behind me. I swear it."

One knight pulled his horse to a stop and pushed up his visor. "Your loss, farmer. Our master especially wanted the one named Arabella who is now calling herself Leah. Women." He snorted. "The silly wench thought changing her name would fool us." He held out one armored hand to the man. "Your pay is little without her."

Henry turned his agitated horse in a circle and pointed to the trees. "Look up. She has to be up there."

Her betrayer kept pointing up, but the men in full armor had difficulty following his pointing finger. Any movement to look up caused their visors to shut. The metal collars limited their range of motion. One knight, frustrated with his inability to look into the trees, shouted, "Go get her, farmer."

Henry dismounted and with a thunderous countenance strode to a tree, muttering loudly enough for everyone to hear. "She's a witch. She comes and goes as she pleases. One moment she's here, the next she's gone."

Leah invoked the elements to watch over her as she tried to control her shivering. It felt like something was crawling on her skin. Henry looked at all the trees, probably looking for one with branches low enough for her to reach. He strolled to her tree with a triumphant smile.

Mother Earth, help me now," she whispered, rubbing her hands over her arms to discover they felt somewhat rubbery. A quick glance revealed the snake had draped itself over her shoulders. She realized it wasn't her skin that resembled a basketball covering, but the snake's. Her hands wrapped grasped the snake's body. The brownish reptile lay complacent against her, taking advantage of her body heat. She gently lifted the snake and held it in front of her. With a mental apology to the snake, she dropped it without a sound.

The six-foot snake landed on Henry. His screams indicated a fear of snakes, or of unexpected objects falling from trees. The knights laughed as he danced around, trying to free himself from the reptile. The snake wrapped itself around his neck, holding on after its most recent flight. "Do something!"

One knight unsheathed a sword and waved it over his head. "I can cut it from your neck." He demonstrated with a few sweeping arcs of his sword.

The knight looked a little wobbly. Leah was unsure if he was tired or *drunk. Henry must have thought the same, because he yelped, "No sword!"*

The two knights signaled to each other, put down their visors, and galloped off. Henry staggered to a stop and dropped to his knees. "This is how it ends." He fell forward, resting on his elbows. The snake felt close enough to the ground to slither from Henry's neck, making a slow turn through the grass to head back to its tree, which guaranteed Henry would not be climbing it any time soon.

Henry pushed up, threw a malice-filled look at the snake. The lower part of his tunic had darkened with moisture, demonstrating his real fear of reptiles. Nope, Henry definitely wouldn't be climbing up the tree. Obviously, Mother Earth had sent her the snake. Thank the Goddess, it wasn't hurt.

Cursing, Henry swung into the saddle of his horse to follow the other riders. Would he come back and search for her again? Would he assume she'd just vanished since she'd before? Her thighs could only take so much of pretending to be a bird on a wire. The forest sounds of birds calling and animals rustling under the underbrush began to return, assuring her the men were gone.

Reaching to another limb for balance, she pulled herself upright, ignoring her protesting muscles. She'd give them another thirty minutes to get out of the area, but she needed to get moving while there was still daylight.

The brown snake moved slowly up the tree. Leah watched with both gratefulness and trepidation. Couldn't say she'd ever been fond of snakes, but then again, she'd never had any experience with them, either. This snake had saved her life. It really was a very special snake. As if reading her thoughts, the snake made its way to her branch. It slithered up to her and stopped. The lower half of its body twined around the branch, the other half, which included the head, rose to look in her direction as if trying to communicate.

Lowering carefully back down to her haunches, she reached out a hand to lightly touch the reptile's head. "Thank you, Brother Snake. I owe you."

A light of recognition shone in its beady eyes. Its tongue slid out, tasted the air, and withdrew into its mouth.

Leah kept her hand on the serpent's head deciding it wasn't that scary at all. "I'm sorry for throwing you. I understand now we're all pearls on a string."

An impression of flight, then a sudden ending of flight filled her mind. Her mouth dropped open. Could she read the snake's mind? Jerking her hand back, she considered the snake. Could it tell her which way to go? She doubted it.

Standing gingerly, she stepped carefully over the snake. Using the branches, she backed her way down the tree until she got to the last branch and had to jump. No clue, which way to go, she reached for the pendant Nana had given her. Fisting her fingers around it, she prayed for guidance. Gaia, you're strength is strong in this world. Please guide me." The sun appeared to be on its descent. In that case, she'd head to the east, the direction of new beginnings.

CHAPTER TWELVE

*T*HE BIRDS CALLED *out to one another as she made her way through the undergrowth. Shoes would have been beneficial. Of course, back when she'd been in her house she hadn't had to worry about shoes. "Ouch," she yelped, and hopped. A nearby sapling held her up as she examined her foot. A good-size thorn had imbedded itself in her big toe. Luckily, there was enough base for her to pull it out. Blood trickled out of the wound. Not good. Even she knew walking on it in the dirt would cause an infection. Who knew what medieval germs might do to her? Possibly give her some disease they'd managed to eliminate through vaccinating generations of people.*

Some antibiotic cream would have come in handy. Better yet, a bandage would have been nice. Remembering hearing something about saliva being helpful in the healing process, Leah spat in her hand and rubbed the spit on her toe. All the spit did was rub off some dirt. She couldn't walk on a bleeding foot. Leah used the edge of her robe to apply pressure, which was challenging since she'd to keep her balance in a semi-crouched position on one foot. Mentally, she counted off the seconds. By the time she got to ten, she realized sitting down would make it easier. Letting go of her injured toe, she balanced on the heel of her hurt foot as she eased herself to the ground.

Holding her robe down, she made sure the fabric touched the ground protecting her skin. The last thing she needed was poison ivy on her butt. That would have been grand, as if things weren't already. Cross-legged, she was better able to examine her toe. Her thumb felt for the hole. Not finding it, she pulled her foot closer to her face. Nope, nothing, except a clean spot on her big toe, but that couldn't be right. It had to have been the other foot. Pulling up the opposing foot, she examined it, which was filthy. Employing her spit method, she cleaned the other toe, which looked fine.

Okay. Neither toe had a hole. She wiggled both toes. Both toes worked, and there was no pain. Had she stepped on a thorn? Had she imagined all of this? Was she starting to lose her mind? It might be a result of traveling through time rapidly. Leah placed her hands behind her for support, she rested as she considered the various scenarios. Right now, she could be in a padded room to keep her from hurting herself. None of this was real, not even the mild discomfort in her right palm. Pulling up her right hand, she looked at it. Pressed into it was a dirty, bloody thorn.

It hadn't pierced the skin. Apparently, it had been lying on the ground where she'd thrown it after extracting it from her toe. She held it up close to her. The blood was still wet on the thorn. The palm of her hand bore the impression of the thorn and a smear of blood. It had happened. She wasn't in a padded room somewhere. The only thing she'd done, other than clean it with her saliva, was use her robe to staunch the bleeding. It had to be the robe, didn't it?

Never a big one for pain, she forced herself to test her hypothesis. Jabbing the dirty thorn into her palm enough to pierce the skin, she watched it bleed before applying the robe to it. Concentrating, she felt the pain leave and the skin heal. Dropping the robe, she examined her unpierced palm. "Whoa, who knew?" Actually, she did. Nana was full of mysterious healings, and apparently magickal garments, too.

Still, this was the first time she'd experienced it. At home, when they'd wrapped her in bandages with the cream, she'd been so weary all she'd done was sleep. She'd believed she'd whip marks on her body because Stella, Nana, and Mother had assured her she did. She saw them too. Just a few minutes ago, she hadn't paid attention to when her toe stopped hurting, focused on leaving the woods before dark. This time, she knew. She'd felt the healing.

She'd witnessed the magick. This changed everything.

Gingerly, she put her formerly injured foot down and felt no pain. That was good. Still, it was hard to get her mind around a magickal healing robe. Fingering the fabric, she continued eastward. The robe was attractive with all the blues and greens in it. Looking like leaves sometimes and flames when she looked it again. Occasionally, it flashed silver, but that color had somehow dulled when she'd crouched in the tree. You would think everyone would want robe so special that it clung to her when climbing or running to stay out of the way. No underbrush caught on it, either. It was almost as if it moved away.

Those thirteen women versed in the nature-based religions had each held her robe and put some version of themselves into it. They'd whispered incantations and invoked protection from the various goddesses. Since Nana's group was not pro-god, they only believed in the Divine Feminine, so they never bothered to call on any gods. Her father could have invoked the Lord of the Forest to look over her. He'd sent the snake.

Up to now, she'd been ready to distance herself from her family's faith to give herself a better chance to date Dylan. Wow, it made her wonder if this trip into the past had been more for the current Leah, than her past life as Arabella. Overall, she didn't really like Arabella much, but she tried to remember she was a product of her time. Emotions, motives, and actions that didn't jive with her present-day interpretations weren't necessarily wrong for this time.

A bunny darted in front of her. It sat and looked at her for a moment, showing no fear. This was odd, considering bunnies often ended up in stew pots in this century. Its casual attitude might have been more understandable in her neighborhood, where all the rabbits had to fear was a half-hearted chase by an overfed pooch. They usually outsmarted the dog by standing still, since dogs chased only things that moved.

The hare hopped forward about a foot, then turned to look at her. It stared at her with its gentle brown eyes. Leah took a step toward the creature. The bunny hopped a few more feet, then looked at her again. It acted as if it wanted her to follow. How weird was that? She took another step. The bunny glanced over its shoulder to make sure she still followed. After a while, it quit looking, confident Leah had finally gotten with the program.

The light in the woods grew dimmer as birds found their perches to roost for the night. Leah knew the nocturnal animals would be out soon. What ran around at night in the woods? True, she was a city girl, but she did take biology. Raccoons, possums, and owls tended to dominate the night, with the occasional shrew, mouse, and rat. A shudder ran through her at the thought of rats. Wait a minute? Didn't rabbits come out at dawn and dusk, too? This little fellow had come out early.

She considered the white-tailed bunny in front of her. It was an enchanted bunny, so that made sense. Enchanted? Really, those words were in her head. Better yet, she accepted them as if she were in a fairy tale. What if the harmless little bunny was leading her astray and taking her to some place evil?

Henry was a bunny, in a way. She'd trusted him, never thought he would hurt her. Yep, she remembered how that turned out. Barking sounded in the distance. Had the villagers returned with dogs to hunt for her? Another bark answered the first one. Then there seemed to be a chorus. Not dogs. She'd watched Dracula *enough to recognize the children of the night, wolves. Hurry bunny. Get us there. The rabbit increased its speed, which made sense, since rabbits were a wolf delicacy.*

They broke into a clearing where a neat little cottage sat surrounded by a wood fence. Glancing at the smoke curling out of the chimney, she wondered who lived there. A child brought up on Grimm's fairy tales would expect an evil witch, but she knew better. Nana had let her know most fairy tales scared kids into appropriate behavior. Children wandering off into the woods could end up as dinner for large predators. The thought had her swinging open the gate and hoping for the best. The bunny hopped in step with her, which didn't surprise her.

The door opened. A tall, bearded man stood in the door. Leah bit her lip, taking in the man, trying to decide if she could trust him. Everyone in this century had proved to be unreliable, always out for themselves, unlike in her century, where the intentions were the same, but people at least tried to hide them. His eyes were alert, intelligent. He allowed her to take his measure before smiling. "So have you decided yet if you can trust me?"

How did he know? He'd sent the bunny. She looked around for the bunny, but it was gone. A man, a teen really, walked around the side of the cottage, attired in a tunic, drying his face. His brown hair was a bit unkempt and long. He lowered the towel and smiled when the bearded man praised him.

"Good job, Simon, leading my granddaughter home."

Granddaughter? She looked at the bearded man and tried to see the dapper man depicted in the pictures Nana had showed. His hair and beard were white, which time and living here would have affected. Her head swiveled to regard Simon, whose eyes appeared to have an interested gleam. Still, they were the same soft brown as the rabbit's.

Her grandfather? It felt weird calling him that. He flourished a walking stick and reached past her to rap Simon on the shoulder. "Take care to remember she is my granddaughter."

The teen colored, hung his head, and murmured, "Sorry, Master."

Master? This was becoming stranger and stranger. Was Simon a slave?

Her grandfather stood aside and motioned her in. "Come in, come in, I will answer all your questions. I bet your mother calls you Leah."

"How did you know?" This man she'd never met before could not only read her thoughts, but he knew about her.

He chuckled. "All in good time. Have a seat." Two chairs sat near the fireplace, where a large dog dozed.

She sat in one while she watched her newfound grandfather dip a cup into a bucket of water to fill a kettle. After several cups of water, he hooked the kettle on an iron arm that he swung over the fire. "We'll have tea in no time," he commented, as he turned to sit.

Leah cataloged all the changes in him since his last photograph. She'd had no clue he'd be so wizardly looking with his long beard and hair.

"I know you have questions. You may wonder why you can't read my thoughts. Well, I've walls in place as do most good ceremonial magicians."

Actually, she hadn't thought that far. She tried to open her mind to see if she could receive anything. A weak message came to her, but not in her grandfather's voice. Something about her being beautiful, special...she preened at those words, until they were followed by "sure she's not wearing anything under her robe." Her head swiveled as she pinned Simon with a glare, obviously the source of the thoughts.

Grandfather stood, pointing his index finger at the door. "Out," he shouted in Simon's direction. "Stay out until you have control of your thoughts. I taught you better than that."

Simon scurried out of the house, his actions reminiscent of the rabbit. Grandfather shook his head. "He shows great promise, but still he's an adolescent male, and when faced with a beautiful girl his mind tends to run to the earthy side. Forgive him for my sake. There's much to like about him."

Leah nodded her head. It wasn't as if Simon had been the first boy to ever ogle her. She wasn't offended. The ability to read people's minds perplexed and intrigued her. Would she be able to know the answers for a test without studying for it? Would she understand people better? "Grandfather, you can read people's minds. Is it helpful?"

His teeth flashed in his beard. "The sad truth is most of what people think is not worth knowing. Humans must be the whiniest creatures alive. There's a lot of 'I'm tired,' 'I'm hungry,' 'this is too hard,' 'that's unfair.' When They're't whining, They're hatching plots against one another for gain, sometimes revenge and, in some cases, love, but that's only what they call it. A person never hatches a scheme to snare love. It happens, one of the grandest occurrences in the universe."

Her plan to tap into her teachers' minds flamed out. She could do without knowing a teacher hated his job, had missed breakfast, or wore contacts that were bothering him. The last part about love had caught her attention. "If love is one of the grandest occurrences in the universe, why did you leave Nana?"

"Esmeralda." He said the name and placed a hand over his heart. "Is she still spitting fire?"

Leah had almost forgotten her grandmother's real name. She always called her Nana, her mother referred to her as Mother, while friends all called her Baba Esme. "Daily. I'm not too sure if she'll be thrilled you're alive or will be ready to beat you with a stick. Can we go now and find out?"

Grandfather shook his head as he swung the kettle off the fire. Lifting the lid, he threw in a handful of leaves. "Ah, it's not that easy, little one. I came to this time when I divined one of my grandchildren would have need of me. The portals of time aren't always easy to find or to open. Twenty years ago, I found this one and knew it might be my only chance to help you."

If her grandfather had willingly gone into the past, why did she keep going back and forth? "It makes no sense to me. You wanted to be here and used your skills to find your way here. I don't want to be here, but I keep coming back. Why is that?"

Her grandfather stood to lift two mugs from the shelf. He poured steaming, fragrant tea into each cup and handed her one. "There's no real access to sugar, but I can offer you honey." He held out a small earthen pitcher to her.

She drizzled some into her tea, realizing Grandfather hadn't answered her question. She placed the cup to her lips and tasted the aromatic tea. It was quite delicious, even though she wasn't much of a tea lover. Everything wasn't bad in the past.

His eyebrows beetled down as he spoke. "I've given a great deal of thought and research to this. Because I'm here in this time, I witnessed the courtship and love of Arabella and Lionel and the corruption of that love for evil."

"Did you actually see it?" She imagined her grandfather in the bushes while Lionel offered his wildflower bouquet to Arabella.

"Ah, you'd make a Peeping Tom out of me." He sipped from his mug. He sighed and then gestured to a dark mirror leaning against the wall. "I used my scrying mirror to see them. I felt Arabella's soul, and I knew it was part of my future granddaughter. This was the reason I came. In a way, I spied on the two of them, but I needed knowledge to help you."

Leah wondered why he hadn't helped her when she was hiding in the trees from the peasants. Why hadn't he helped her when they'd lashed her? What about when she was hiding from Henry? Her gaze darted to the man sitting across from her. He'd already demonstrated he could read her thoughts.

"Ah, little one, I've helped you as much as I could. I cannot leave this place." He gestured to the room. "I cannot even step outside the fence. This time portal is my home until it blinks out of existence in three days. In that time, I will be transported back to my dear Esmeralda."

Her mind caught on the facts that he'd helped her and that he would transport back in three days. "When you go, I want to be with you."

"That's my plan." He leaned forward to pat her hand affectionately.

Leah considered him. He seemed nice and rather what you'd expect in a grandfather. Well, if your grandfather happened to be a ceremonial magician. "How did you help me?"

"Harumpft." He cleared his throat, clearly bristling at the implication that she doubted him. "As you know, I cannot leave this place, but I could see what was happening. Do you think the men and their dog turned away per chance? No, I put the fear of the tree folks in their heads. As for your lashing, it was a gentle one. Most people die from it. I held the wrist of the flogger, making it hard for him to put much force into his swing. He was a brute. It wasn't easy, let me tell you." He pointed to his head as an explanation of how he'd accomplished such a feat.

Leah thought she understood. "The snake I threw on Henry. That was you, too. Was the snake Simon?"

Her grandfather laughed. "Simon would not like to hear you liken him to a snake. No, that was Horace."

"Is he another apprentice?" How many did her grandfather have?

"No, Horace is a snake. I've become very familiar with the woodland creatures with my time here. I've named most of them. I'm not sure if I'm ready to socialize with regular folks." He pursed his lips and looked into the fire.

Her grandfather had willingly given up so much for a granddaughter he'd never met because of something he'd seen in his scrying mirror. His faith and love had to be absolute. She wished she'd both.

Setting his cup down, he looked at her. "It will come. I imagine you want to hear the story about Lionel and Arabella."

CHAPTER THIRTEEN

*L*EAH WANTED TO *hear their story. In a way, it was her story, too. Often, souls re-enacted the same scenes from past lifetimes until they managed to get it right. Some reincarnation theories believed you met the same souls from previous lifetimes in other bodies, which explained why you might meet a total stranger and have an immediate dislike for them. On the other hand, you could meet a spouse or a lover from an earlier lifetime and feel an immediate pull.*

The door opened, allowing a rush of cool air and a sliver of darkness in, along with Simon. He sat near enough for Leah to notice his thoughts consisted of her being the granddaughter of the great wizard. He was trying. She'd give him that. Grandfather acknowledged him with a nod but continued speaking.

"Lionel's family was the only noble family in the area. There were some successful merchants, but no other nobles nearby. It wasn't surprising that Lionel played with the local children. As a boy and the third son, he was of little importance." Grandpa stopped long enough to stare into his cup with a frown, and he reached for the kettle to pour more tea into his mug.

Leah thought about her little brother, who was the third child and a boy. No way you could have ignored him. As if he would ever let you. "Why didn't they pay much attention to him?"

"In noble families, it is all about passing on the name. You need male children to do that."

Leah snorted her thoughts on the custom, but circled her hand for him to continue when Grandfather looked at her questioningly.

"The heir and the spare, they like to call the first two sons. The first one takes over the title and the estate. The second trains for the military. Reginald went to school to learn how to run the estate and make the important connections he needed with other first sons. Archibald, the second son, went to a different household to learn to be a knight. This ensured more connections for the family. The more connections you have, the better off you're. In a time of attack or need, you can call on your connections."

Simon spoke out, startling Leah because she'd forgotten he was there. "Boys must learn a craft to survive. Farming is for the firstborn because the land goes to the firstborn. No land grants in my family."

Leah turned to look at the young man sitting cross-legged on the floor. "Did you decide you wanted to be a wizard and searched for my grandfather?"

Simon looked down as he answered, making his reply a little hard to hear. "The miller was my master. He found fault with my work and beat me."

Grandfather explained more. "He ran into the woods and became lost. He wandered for days, hungry and hurt. Simon was fearful to return to the miller, who would beat him more for deserting his post. I sent a wild creature out to bring him to me."

Simon made a rueful expression, mumbling something about a pack of wolves.

A smile flitted across Grandfather's face as he regarded the sullen boy. "The wolves were my last resort. I sent birds, a raccoon, even a bunny, but you ignored them all."

"Not true," Simon complained. "I tried to catch the hare for supper."

Grandfather shook his head. "That was two or three years ago. Simon has become a talented apprentice in the intervening time. Where was I in the story?"

"You were…" both Simon and Leah started together. Simon gestured for her to continue.

"The part about Lionel and how his family didn't pay too much attention to him," Leah prompted.

Stroking his beard for a moment, his eyes glittered with amusement. "I was trying to remember what things were like back in the twentieth century. Children were kings whose parents carted them around to numerous events for their benefit. Parents trumpeted their achievements, no matter how minor, as if they were gods who'd managed to create a new planet. Are things still about the same?"

"Worse in some ways," Leah admitted, wrinkling her nose as if she smelled something nasty.

"Here in this time, people do not fuss over their children. They try to avoid attachment because many die before five years of age. Often, the children don't get a name until they turn two."

Leah hated interrupting, but she'd to know. "Why don't they name the children?"

Simon volunteered the information with enthusiasm. "You're often named after someone in the family. If the child dies, the name is wasted."

"So for a while," Grandfather continued as if not interrupted, "most children roam free. For non-noble children, there might be chores to do to help maintain the household, but adult life comes fast. Boys often apprentice as young as ten. While girls often marry as early as twelve. Lionel had more freedom than most with no chores to bind him and an indulgent mother. Both her other sons were sent away, and she wanted to hold on to this last son as long as she could. Since he was for the church, once he left she might not see him again or very seldom. Her oldest would manage the estate. Her second born could visit between battles, but once the church has you, it's as if you have no family."

Leah thought it sounded rather ominous, rather like going to prison. She said nothing because she did not want to interrupt the tale.

"Lionel knew all the children of the village. His kind manner made him a favorite of the girls, along with his handsome appearance. The boys tolerated him. To do otherwise would have resulted in repercussions to their families. He must have sensed this. He spent less and less time rough housing with the boys and more time with the girls, especially Arabella. Most everyone in the village knew they were special friends. Her family warned Arabella not to make too much of it, while hoping there might be a way to gain from an alliance."

Sucking in her lips, Leah knew there was a hidden message there. "I don't understand."

"Ahh," Grandfather breathed the word as he obviously stalled. "Girls are not considered valuable in this time. The best you can do with a girl child is to broker good marriage to increase your wealth or connections. Even though Arabella was a pretty child, they didn't expect Lionel to marry her. He was noble and intended for the church. His family held to the Catholic faith. Priests don't marry. Still, they also wondered about the possibility of a child. If Lionel had a child with Arabella, it would be a child of noble blood. His family would feel obligated to take care of it, especially his mother. This was risky, but they knew Lionel's mother well. She'd relish another child."

"What?" Leah may have raised her voice. "I don't get it. They wanted their daughter to be little more than a teen mom."

Simon watched the words fly between her and her grandfather and grinned. Was he smiling because Leah was so ignorant of the morals of this time? She decided against scanning his mind, afraid of what she might find.

Grandfather picked up the kettle and indicated her cup. She held it out as he poured and talked. "This was only an option. It never occurred. Still, there was deep affection between Arabella and Lionel. First love on Lionel's part, while Arabella's love grew in absentia."

"That makes no sense. How could she love him more when he was gone?"

Leah wondered, since she often heard people tended to forget crushes once they left the scene.

"Keep in mind, she was young when Lionel left, not ready for marriage, but she'd eventually have to marry. Her family encouraged several different suitors, good men with portions to ensure a decent life for the fair Arabella, but she chose none of them. She claimed none were as sweet, handsome, or as thoughtful as Lionel. Desperate families often resort to desperate measures. Arabella was developing a name as a difficult woman because she'd chosen none of her suitors. Still, she was the most beautiful woman in the area, which caused the single women of the village to dislike her. Ah, women. Are they still the same in your time, Leah?"

She was tempted to say worse, thinking of Cerberus, the three mean girls in her time, but she was unsure how bad the women in this time were. "What happened to Lionel?"

Simon leaned forward to comment. "They bundled him off to church, did they not?"

"They did," Grandfather acknowledged. "There was much weeping and gnashing of teeth from both Lionel and his mother. It was not a pretty scene, which only reassured his sire it was past time for Lionel to join the good brothers. The church, especially the Catholic one, has nothing good to say about women. In fact, they credit them with sin, temptation, and any other evil. Inside the cloistered walls, Lionel's heart was hardened against his former love."

"I saw it." Leah wanted to share the details of her dream or vision with someone who'd understand and would be better able to explain it to her. "Lionel sat with an abbot, I think. He poured water into a silver-lined bowl and did some sort of divination for Lionel. In it, he showed Arabella playing him false with some bearded man. I knew at the time this was a conjured image. Later, he offered Lionel wine in which he stirred in some powder."

"The Black Abbot is a bad one for sure. His heart is against all humankind, but he also uses the magickal arts to promote his own greed for power and wealth. He probably strangled puppies as a boy."

The thought made her shudder. "Isn't he a priest? I didn't think they believed in spells and magick."

"There has always been magick. There are even laws on the books about not using magic for nefarious purposes. It is still there for people who care to research. Ironically, in the last hundred and fifty years, people managed to forget this. All our current Christian holidays were originally rituals to welcome seasons, to encourage fertility, to show gratitude.

The Catholic Church printed out pamphlets showing lurid depictions of people tortured by witches and demons to turn people against everyday intentional magick. This encouraged people's natural fears. It also stamped out the earth magick people used to hunt and plant crops. Who would want to suffer a painful, ignoble death as a witch?" Grandfather's expression appeared unfocused.

Wiping his eyes with his hand, he said, "Religion has always been used to manipulate the populace for the benefit of one or two people. People swarm to do their bidding, expecting a heavenly reward or afraid of a hellish torment. Too many good people have died in the name of religion. Their only crime was they were in the way." He sighed deeply and folded his hands.

Leah wondered if that was the end of the tale. Was there more? She wanted to understand the part she played. Should she ask? She hated to bother her grandfather, who appeared to be off on another plane. Maybe he was witnessing the deaths of those who'd managed to get in the way of new dominant religions. It always amazed her how people never seemed to have a clue how religions came and went, often having the same claims as the previous ones. Still, this particular one involved her life and her ability to continue to live in the twenty-first century as opposed to dying in some medieval backwater village.

"I hear you, child." Grandfather pinned her with his intense stare. "I'm *sorry for your suffering. In this time and the other, I've done what I could. I could not prevent all harm to you or Arabella. For that, I apologize."*

His ominous words gave her goose bumps on her arms, and her stomach rolled. *"Do I die here?"*

"Arabella dies here, as she should because people do not live forever. Her death can be meaningful, as opposed to just another statistic, just another woman accused of being a witch. There are no creatures as evil as the witch catchers are. They defame, humiliate, torture, and kill in the name of religion." He turned to spit in the direction of the fire.

Okay. Arabella died in this time, which she understood. Her issue was that people kept confusing her for Arabella. Was Arabella running around at this time, too? Did Leah somehow take her place? Was she supposed to make some bold statement to Lionel before she died? She understood less than she'd before. She'd the feeling she'd never get to go out with Dylan. It had nothing to do with him liking her, but more to do with being alive.

"Grandfather, I'm not sure what happens to me. I'm not sure if I take Arabella's place. Do we exist at the same time? Am I inside Arabella, looking out? If so, do I die with Arabella? I don't want to die." Her voice trembled as she spoke the words. She tried not to cry, but a few tears slipped out.

"Ah, my sweet, precious granddaughter," he said and stood. Grabbing her hand, he pulled her into his embrace. *"I came here to rescue you."*

He fingered the sleeve of her robe. *"Look at this gown of yours. It crackles with protection magick so heavy it would sear a normal man."* He pointed to the medallion. *"I never thought to see that necklace off Esmeralda's neck. There are centuries of magic in that one charm. Do not underestimate the power in yourself. Then there's the most powerful magick of all."* He tightened his embrace.

She hated to ask, certain she should know the answer. *"What is this powerful magick?"*

He loosed his embrace, stepped back, and gazed at her in surprise. *"Real-*

ly, Leah? The most powerful magick is love. Even though the abbot did his best to turn Lionel's love into hate, he still wants to love her. Remind him of that love."

"I don't know." Turning her back on her grandfather, she began to pace the small room, skirting the still-seated Simon. "I think this is too hard for me. Why can't someone else do it?"

"Trust me, Leah. I've tried everything I've known and have improvised a few other things I wasn't too sure of, but nothing changed. This is not my destiny. It's yours." His voice and manner were solemn, giving his words an air of finality.

It looked like there was no way to get out of this. It was similar to the time she'd transferred to a new school the day they were doing the presidential fitness challenge. It hadn't mattered that she'd just gotten over the flu. She'd still had to do it. Of course, this was ten times worse. "Can you promise I won't die?"

"No."

The one word settled on her like a weight, stopped her pacing, and pressed her to the ground. He wasn't supposed to say that. Didn't he have a clue what grandfathers were supposed to be like? Where were his words of cheer?

Grandfather walked to where she'd collapsed and held out his hand. It was obvious she could expect no coddling. She often thought of herself as an adult. It was time to start acting like one. She took his hand and allowed him to pull her up. He ushered her back to the chair and waited until she sat before resuming his seat.

"I've done the calculations, consulted the stars, and even used my scrying mirror without any definite results. There are three possibilities." He held up his index finger.

"You do whatever it is you're supposed to do and then return to me at this cottage. We blink back to modern time together."

That sounded good. She could do that. "And the others?"

He held up two fingers. "The second is you do whatever is needed, and you blink back into your time the way you have before. I follow through the portal."

"Okay. I'm good with that." Then there was the third possibility. It would probably be the one she liked the least. "What is the third?"

"Ah, yes, that one." Grandfather stalled by beetling his brows, flaring his nostrils, and finally he spoke. "You die here."

That one she liked the least. No doubt about it.

Shaking his head, he apologized. "I'm sorry to upset you. It is better to be prepared. This may be the mission of your existence, the reason you were born."

She'd hoped for something better, even the opportunity to fall in love, have a career, and possibly be a mother. Dying in the wrong century in a case of mistaken identity had never ever entered her mind. "I was hoping to do something noble, like cure cancer," she attempted to joke.

"I understand," he said. "If you're successful, many lives could be saved. These senseless killings will be stopped."

Leah was more concerned about one life, hers. Would it be petty to want to live if she could prevent others from dying? You might as well call her petty. "What is this thing I do to prevent others from dying?"

"I'm glad you asked." Her grandfather tried for a smile but failed. His expression took on a painful mien. "You have to convince Lionel he's been tricked, led astray with all these tales of witches killing babies, drinking the blood of sleeping people, and flying through the night."

"He actually believes that?" It was hard for Leah to accept. True, there were times she wished she could fly.

Her grandfather nodded, before continuing.

"There's one problem. Lionel is some type of addict. He looks horrible. I'd call him a meth head only I don't think it has happened yet. His pupils

are tiny even in low light. He has bags under his eyes. His skin is sallow and just hangs on his skinny body. When he talks, it is sometimes hard to understand him, which just makes him angrier. Everyone knows you can't reason with an addict." Did her grandfather think she'd superhuman powers? The last noble thing she'd done was stand up for Jeremy, and that had been impulsive. If she'd thought it out, she'd never have done it.

"That does sound like an addict, which can be good and bad. Their minds tend to drift, which makes it hard for him to keep focused on killing witches. On the other hand, the abbot probably motivates him with additional fixes. The bad thing is reaching him in a coherent moment."

Did that make things better? Actually, no. She sucked in her lips, wondering what she should do. "The drug is mixed in wine. If he is not drinking wine, he should be okay." She knew better, but tried to find a tiny window of hope.

"Maybe." Grandpa said the word in a considering manner as he stroked his long beard. "You must convince him you still love him and that you waited for his return. Let him know he's mistaken about the witches. There's a small problem, though, which will make him doubt you."

This didn't sound good. Instinct told her not to ask, but it was better to be prepared than ambushed. "The problem is?"

"You're pregnant."

"I'm pregnant!" She patted the gown over her flat stomach. "I can assure you I'm not pregnant. I know what is required to create a baby. Trust me, it hasn't occurred. We move too much for it to happen. Technically, I haven't even been on an actual date."

"Not you. Arabella. When Lionel looks at you, he'll see Arabella, big with child. That is the reason she is still alive. The child is innocent of the mother's crimes, so Arabella cannot be killed until she delivers."

Great. This was worse than a soap opera. "Is it Lionel's child?"

"No." Her grandfather shook his head. "Arabella was raped, which is

not too uncommon considering how pretty she is. You can tell him the truth. He might believe you. Rape is quite common, as is sexual abuse."

Every word her grandfather spoke made her mission even more impossible. *"Okay, here's what I have. My job is to convince Lionel of my enduring love while my belly is big with some other man's child. I also have to convince him the religion he's pledged his life to is misguided and is killing innocent people. Is that about it?"*

"Keep in mind, many thousands are directing intention energy your way," her grandfather reminded.

Way to pile on the guilt. *I will be letting down thousands if I don't sacrifice myself.* She used her sleeve to wipe the cold sweat off her forehead. *"It will be a piece of cake,"* she said, knowing she'd never spoken a bigger lie in her life.

CHAPTER FOURTEEN

*L*EAH SLEPT IN *her grandfather's bed that night, despite her protests. The sight of both her grandfather and Simon sleeping on the hard-packed dirt floor in front of the fire made her feel guilty for taking the only bed. Simon explained he usually slept on the floor, except when he chose to sleep outside, and then he slept on the ground. It wasn't too bad for Simon. He was young and used to it, but Grandpa was old, probably seventy.*

The pine needles managed to work their way through the thin mattress covering when they could and ended up sticking her. At least the mattress smelled good. It reminded her of the floor cleaner her mother used. Unfortunately, the rope bed with the pine-needle mattress was rather uncomfortable. Every time she moved, the ropes protested, as if they might break any moment. It was hard to get comfortable, not only with the bed, but knowing in the morning, she'd have to confront her death or near-death.

A roll had her facing the wall. If she didn't see the crude furniture, the open-hearth fire, the elderly man sleeping on the floor with his apprentice, then she could pretend she was home and be able to fall sleep. Her pillow, filled with dry grass, made a rustling sound when she moved. It wasn't uncomfortable, but the sound was disconcerting. It reminded her of the sound she might hear if a snake was slithering through the grass.

Forcing her eyes shut, she began to count. Sometimes it worked at home. Usually, by the time she got to two hundred, her numbers became confused as she drifted off. This time, no such luck. By thirty, she turned and looked at the semi-curled form of her grandfather. The man had committed almost a third of his life waiting for her in this primitive, dangerous place. She managed to start again and made it to sixty-four before Dylan's face crept into her thoughts. Oh, Dylan, we never even explored what was between us. *Did he wonder where she was? How many days of school had she really missed? Had her mother called the school and explained her daughter was out of the country, no, make that the country and century. She doubted it.*

Would it be small and petty of her to want to go to her junior prom as opposed to changing beliefs and righting wrongs in whatever century this was? If so, she was petty, not to mention scared, very scared. Each trip into the past had terrified her, but until grandfather had explained, she'd never realized she could die here. It was more like watching a scary movie that frightened you in the moment but became less and less frightening the further away from it you got. Only, this wasn't a movie with an automatic happy ending.

Were there ever happy endings? That would imply you were glad something ended. If a woman married her sweetheart, they called it true love. What was ending? The courtship? Many women would deplore that ending. She yawned, blinking her suddenly heavy eyes. Had Grandfather put something in the tea? Suddenly, she felt very, very sleepy.

Leah woke to sunlight streaming in the window and the sound of birds singing. For a moment, a brief second, she thought everything was right in the world. It was Sunday, and she could sleep late. Her father always cooked a hearty breakfast on the weekends, since the family could eat together. He'd wake her up when it was time.

"Leah," a male voice whispered close to her ear. It was familiar but not her father's. An elderly, bearded man with concerned eyes leaned over her. Who was he? It all came back at once, hitting her with the same impact as when the neighbor's over-friendly Great Dane had jumped on her. The dog had never had a grasp on how big he was.

She held her head straight, bit her bottom lip, and wondered if she could think herself home. Nana always preached to her the value of intention. A person could do anything if they just believed. Right now, she believed she wanted to be home. If she didn't turn her head to see the primitive cabin, she hadn't be here. She could return to the world where her sheets smelled like fabric softener and she dreamed of dancing with Dylan at the junior prom. Technically, she'd have to ask him, since he was a year younger. Like that would ever happen. Her gaze moved around Grandfather to the drying herbs hanging from the beams to Simon squatting in front of the fire, stirring something in a cauldron. Simon turned, caught her attention and said, "Gruel is ready."

Gruel? Was that something people actually ate? It sounded like something from a Dickens novel. It didn't sound appetizing, either. No pancakes or link sausages for her, that's for sure. Her grandfather thanked Simon and turned to her.

"Rise and shine, Leah. Today will be the making of you. Not many have the opportunity to confront their destiny so early in life's journey. This can only mean a special life awaits you full of wonder and possibilities." His yellowed teeth appeared in a wide grin.

She mentally made note of the teeth, and the fact he still had any. It was miraculous. She'd noticed that Margaret had had a fair amount of teeth gone, and she was younger than grandfather was. Her eyes narrowed suspiciously at her grandfather. Did he really believe half of what he said? On the other hand, was he trying to use some form of positive-thinking mumbo jumbo on her?

A slight singed smell permeated the air.

"Make haste," Simon urged as he swung the small cauldron up to the table.

He used a ladle to scoop out a light gray substance that had the consistency of soup into three carved, wooden bowls. Even though she was hungry, she doubted she could stomach it. "Um, what exactly is in it?"

Her grandfather opened a small box from which he took a pinch and sprinkled on his food. "It's better with salt, but since salt is hard to come by, we use it sparingly." Both Simon and Grandfather dug into their own bowls with vigor. In fact, they held up their bowls and drank the mixture.

Leah took a pinch of salt, hoping it would change the food into something edible.

Grandfather continued to eat, but he paused to notice Leah not eating. "Eat up, child. It is nothing harmful. Rather like cereal, it is a mixture of rye, millet, and sometimes oats. We're fortunate because Simon has proven himself very adept at relocating bags of grain at the miller's place. Some folks have to subsist on gruel made from tree bark."

The cooling bland cereal mixture sat in her mouth. It reminded her slightly of a breakfast cereal her mother had cooked for her when she was young, determined she'd have a hot breakfast before school. At the time, she'd assumed her mother was a bad cook. It had never occurred to her it was supposed to taste that way. She did remember not liking it, and her mother had let her return to cold cereal. Grandfather calmly mentioning that Simon had stolen the ingredients almost had her spewing her mouthful across the table. Instead, she made herself swallow.

The dog nudged her leg under the table reminding her that it would happily finish her breakfast. It was a thought, but she immediately dismissed it as rude.

Simon put his bowl down. His face bright with delight, he thumped his chest. "The look-away spell confuses my old master, who cannot fathom where the grain goes. Truth is, he steals much on his own. Too much and people begin to suspect."

Grandfather put down his spoon, cocked his head, and gave Leah a long look, before chuckling. "Did you think I conjured up groceries?"

"Truthfully, I never thought about it." She closed her eyes and swallowed another spoon of gruel. The substance would provide her with the nourishment she'd need to accomplish her mission. She figured the slightly burnt taste was her reward for lingering too long in bed. Simon served her grandfather cheerfully, but that had been for only two years or so.

"Grandfather, what did you do before Simon? How did you obtain what you needed?" Obviously, he'd or he wouldn't be looking reasonably healthy today.

He nodded at his apprentice with an indulgent smile. "There have been more than a few lost travelers in the woods. Some didn't show the aptitude or willingness of young Simon. Most longed to return to the more populated towns. A few I graduated to working on their own."

At last, she finished her bowl of gruel. Simon, waiting for such a moment, dolloped more gruel into her bowl with a grin. Great, she'd have to eat that, too. Reaching for the salt, she wondered aloud, "Weren't you afraid of these former visitors leading the witch catchers back to your cottage?"

"Leah, Leah, did my sweet wife tell you so little of me?" He shook his head in disbelief.

"No, absolutely nothing. We could not speak your name. Even to make the mistake of mentioning it in passing would send Nana to her room, where she'd weep for days." He didn't need to know his wife had retired with a fifth of brandy.

"My poor Esmeralda, she didn't know. I could not tell her. One day I looked into the mirror. I saw the portal and you and knew I had mere minutes to reach the portal before it blinked out of existence. Your grandmother had left to do a bit of shopping. I left her a note." His brow beetled, and his lips turned down.

"She never mentioned it. What did the note say?" If he'd left a note, then her grandmother should have understood.

His eyes rolled up in his head as he tried to remember. "It was something about having to do something. That's it."

Really? He considered that a note? "No wonder she's still mad after all *these years. What type of note is that? You didn't tell her you loved her?"*

"She knew I loved her. Didn't I marry her?" He folded his arms in an effort to look stern.

Men. Why didn't they get it? "She might have believed you loved her once, but leaving made her doubt it. Then there was the cryptic note about going to do something. That could mean anything. Maybe you were going to buy cigarettes."

"No, I only smoke a pipe. She should have known better," he corrected her with an eyebrow lift.

Leah searched her mind for what men of that age would have been going to do. "Could be, she thought you were going to play golf with your buds?"

"I never played golf, cricket, croquet, pool, or even poker," he admitted, almost with pride.

"Geesh, what did you do for fun?" Leah would be the first to admit she did not know the habits of middle-aged men.

"Ah, yes, fun. Sometimes, I would meet other ceremonial magicians. We would engage in divination, trying to penetrate each other's mental barriers, astral projection, and aging spirits," Grandfather concluded with a smile.

Leah wasn't about to admit that none of it sounded like a good time to her. "Why would you want to make ghosts older?"

"Ghosts older," he repeated the words as if confused.

Simon comprehended faster. "Aging spirits."

"Oh, that," Grandfather said, then slapped the table as if it were the funniest thing he'd heard. "The spirits I mean were whisky and brandy. Boniface decided to get into the home-brew business, but spirits taste their best with a little age on them. We often took a detour to his cellar and practiced aging a few casks." His face took on a wistful expression that led Leah to believe they'd probably done more in that cellar than just aging the spirits. It sounded as if some sampling went on, too.

"All the same," she said, trying to explain a woman's outlook to a man,

which just might be an impossible task, *"your vague note could have been misinterpreted to mean you were leaving with some bimbo to head to the Bahamas."*

"Esmeralda wouldn't believe that. She was the only woman for me. If she did believe such nonsense, I would have been very afraid. She's not a woman who forgives easy. I often teased her that her middle name was Payback."

Leah regarded her grandfather and his confused expression over the possibility his wife hadn't understood his note.

He threw up his hands, causing wind to whip through the cabin. *"Notes were not my strong point. Actions are."*

Leah admitted to being impressed. She'd never known anyone who could interact with the elements. All the same, a little breeze would not save her grandfather from the wrath of Nana.

"Oh." He drew out the word as if in sudden realization. *"I will have to woo Esmeralda all over again."*

Great, she'd forgotten her mind was an open book to the only ceremonial magician in their family. *"Grandfather, why can you do so much? You can read my mind. Control the elements. Change Simon into an animal.*

"Before, when I asked if Esmeralda ever mentioned me, I wanted to know if she commented on me being a great ceremonial magician. I was at that time. My life was rich with family, friends, and activities. I even had a job. I estimated risk for an insurance company. I was stupendous. Here, I've nothing to entertain my thoughts but my own magick and me. It has allowed me time to sharpen my skills, to perfect areas formerly lacking. All those travelers and young wizards I interacted with have no memory of me or this place."

He spread his broad-tipped fingers on the table and studied them. *"Which goes to show, Granddaughter, if you look hard enough, you can find some good in everything no matter what?"* He lifted his brows at his own statement, asking a question.

What good would come out of this experience? It would depend on if she survived. "Well." She stalled, hoping the right answer would suddenly enter her mind. A quick survey of her experiences provided some insights. "I found out my family loves me very much. Even the women Nana sometimes quarrels with came to my aid." She held out the wide sleeve of her gown. "My protective garment came through the door with someone."

He nodded his head and gave her a significant look. She didn't need to be a mind reader to know it meant continue. Weren't you supposed to do all this debriefing stuff after the mission was finished? "My friend Stella and I were working on an essay on religious prejudice. I found out she is more predisposed to the Wiccan faith than I ever dreamed. I've hidden my beliefs because I never thought of them as mine. I guess I didn't believe in magick."

Simon jumped up. "Not believe in magick? Your grandfather is the most powerful wizard that has ever existed!" He threw his hands wide, as if to indicate the whole world.

"Thank you, Simon, but I prefer the term ceremonial magician." Grandfather twirled his two index fingers for her to resume her revelations.

Directing her words to both Simon and Grandfather, she said, "I do believe in magick now. I've experienced it. I've seen the results of it. I'm wearing it." She looked at both males and added, "I'm looking at it right now."

Simon whooped with delight. Evidently, no one had ever attributed magick to him in so public a statement.

"I also understand why people did what they did in the Burning Years. We allow others to manipulate our fears. When I return home, I refuse to be captive to my fears. Instead, I will be bold. I will do what I want and make the things I desire a reality." She finished with a hand flourish, excited about all she'd discovered and the new fearless life she'd have.

After running from torch-wielding peasants and dogs, hunted by drunken knights, betrayed by a so-called friend, and whipped by the resident dungeon master, high school didn't seem that frightening—even with Cerberus roaming the halls.

Grandfather steepled his fingers and grinned. "If my wooing of my wife goes well, we can chaperone you and Dylan at your junior prom. Esmeralda and I are quite the dancers."

Leah put her hands on her hips. "You'll have to stop reading my mind."

Assuming a solemn mien, he pushed up from the table, pointing a finger in Leah's face. "You will have to develop mental barriers. I may not be the only one able to read your thoughts. They're so loud they practically shout."

She never thought of others reading her thoughts. That wouldn't be good. What if the bad abbot was around? She didn't know if he would be, but she couldn't take any chances. What if she went back to ordinary times and there were a few who could read her mind? What if Dylan could? Obviously, it didn't matter if her math teacher called her obsessed. Everyone knew whom she liked, including Dylan.

"Can you teach me how to erect these barriers? I know it will be a quick course, but I think it will be useful." After all, she could use all the help she could get.

Simon moved closer to the table. "I could benefit from knowing how to erect such barriers."

Leah ended up snorting when all she really wanted to say was, Amen to that, Brother. Simon, in time, might meet a pleasing witch. It would probably be best if she didn't hear Simon's immediate thoughts.

Grandfather held both hands over his head, allowing them to skim just over his body down to his feet. "While your hands move, think of encasing your body in a white envelope of light."

Leah and Simon watched until they realized they should be doing likewise. They flapped their hands awkwardly through the air, resembling seagulls trying to find a place to roost.

"Not like that," he corrected, pointing to spots in the air. "You've left holes in your envelopes, easy openings for your enemies to breach. Keep moving your hands in a smooth fashion. Start over. When you do, recite after me:

Protect this body

Head to toe

Hand to hand

Foot to foot

Skin and bone

Head and heart"

Leah cast a doubting look. "Really? That's it? No long words, mysterious phrases and such? Not even a word or two of Romany?"

"Ah, I see you've been around Esmeralda too long. Nothing fancy. Anything else is all showmanship. Trust me, Leah. This will get the job done." He circled his hand to get them to start.

The spell reminded her of the protection spells they normally used at the beginning of a ritual. What made this one so different? She wondered as she chanted in unison with Simon.

The whiteness settled on her as if a blanket had been tossed from the ceiling. She picked up her feet, one at a time, allowing the protection to flow underneath. The shield felt heavy and thick, as if white cotton batting covered her body.

Simon asked the question she wanted to. "How does this protect our minds from being read?"

Holding up one finger, Grandfather explained, "First, we must protect the body before we can safeguard the mind. If a soldier ran you through with a lance, protecting your mind really wouldn't matter much. You two are ready. Here are some things to consider. Emotions are loud. Beware of the mind-sweepers who look for strong emotion. It can be love, anger, even fear.

It isusually fear. The first thing you must do is not show fright."

Sure thing, all she'd to do was not look afraid. Leah looked from her grandfather to Simon, then back again. Neither cracked a smile, so it must not have been a joke. "How do you do this?"

"You do it all the time. Think of when you see those girls you call Cerberus, or a strange dog growls at you, or the teacher calls on you and you don't know the answer. What do you do?" His eyes peered intently into hers, as if he were confident of her answer.

Thinking back, she tried to remember what she did. With Cerberus, she never made the mistake of acting as if she cared. With the strange dog, she was casual, pretending she hadn't heard his growl. With the teacher, she tried to act confident. There had been times when she'd actually given the wrong answer, but because she'd acted confident, it had been accepted. "I tried to show no emotion."

Grandfather put his index fingers and thumbs together to form a triangle. "Our defense is triangular in nature. The base is," he wiggled his thumbs to demonstrate, "the lack of any outward show of emotions. There are people and entities, which would feed on your fear. Give them nothing."

Holding up one index finger, he said, "The second part is clearing your mind of all fear."

Just like that, she was supposed to clear her mind of all fear. Yeah, sure, and next she'd fly. She sucked her bottom lip in. Didn't fear keep people alive? While she'd never thought of herself as a fearful person, she'd lived most of her life avoiding things that frightened her, including anxiety about not being accepted at her new school and the alarm of moving again. There was always fear somewhere motivating her. Her head shook side to side as she considered his words.

Simon pointed at her, catching her grandfather's attention. "Yes, Leah. Is there something you want to say?"

Not really. She never wanted attention in class, even if it was a class of two. "Well…" She hesitated, not sure how to make her point. "Fear keeps people alive." She motioned to the fire. "A person learns fire is hot, producing a natural fear of putting his hand in the fire."

Simon agreed with her, but she assumed he was just that type of person who would agree with whoever was speaking.

Grandfather graced her with a thoughtful stare. "The knowledge that fire is hot and that you shouldn't stick your hand in it is just that, knowledge. Knowing a bear could kill you is information. Fear muddles your thinking processes and slows your reactions. Sometimes, it can even kill you."

"Fear kills." She said the words slowly, thinking there may have been times when she'd wondered whether she'd live through a scary episode.

"Yes, often creating mental scenarios that are ten times worse than what could really happen. Sometimes you hear about people having a heart attack when a plane starts to plummet. The plane regains altitude, but the person died because, in his mind, he experienced the crash. The ability to control your fear is often the difference between surviving and not."

The elderly dog sitting by the fire began to growl intermittently. The hair stood up on the dog's shoulders and back.

"Esme hears someone," Simon announced.

The dog lurched to her feet on stiff, arthritic legs and swayed a bit. "You named the dog after Nana?"

Grandfather clapped his hands together for attention, Grandfather announced, "We need to work on our shielding. They're drawing closer. Leah, I would consider it a kindness if you didn't mention the dog's name. Women can be funny about these things. Remember, fear changes nothing. Fear doesn't stop a sword from coming toward you, but it will slow your escape. You must be always thinking of the next step. By thinking of moving forward, you're not trapped in fear."

Esme sniffed by the door and growled. The sound of horses milling about and men shouting to one another penetrated the thin walls. "Grandfather,"

Leah whimpered, trying to still the panic that wanted to creep into her voice.

"Do not worry about them. The whole area is enchanted. All they see is more forest." Clapping his hands together again, he spoke. "The third part of the triangle is mental fences. As we wrap our bodies in protective cocoons, we must guard our minds. Think of fences, brick walls, steel boxes, anything impenetrable that will lock out others. Your mind and thoughts are inside. You can also train yourself to go to safe thoughts to keep your mind busy if you think someone might be scanning your thoughts." His attention strayed to the lone window, where the shadows of the horsed men cut out most of the sunlight.

"Safe memories. Should I be thinking of a time I was safe?" Leah wasn't sure how this helped.

"No, not exactly." He edged closer to the window to peer out. "Making brownies, swimming in the ocean, playing with the dog. These are memories that give no real information, or at least the kind they hope to get."

"Let's practice," he called from his stance at the window. "Set up your triangle. I will be Lionel, and I will try to read your mind."

Leah wasn't sure if Lionel had that capability, but she hesitated mentioning it. Instead, she worked on not showing any fear. Her grandfather waved his hands in a flourish and morphed into a thin, haggard man with dark eyes and a wicked-looking staff with some type of spiked device on the end. Terror definitely sought a return visit. Grabbing the emotion ruthlessly, she sat on it and wrestled it into her mental steel box. Quickly, in her mind, she padlocked the box. Simon showed no fear. The ability to change into anyone was another skill she never knew her grandfather possessed. It could have been very useful if he'd ever left the cottage.

"Simon, son of John, tell me where you hid the witch." He breathed the words in a sinister voice, shaking his strange stick threateningly.

The boy, to his credit, kept his face wiped clean of emotion. "Sir, I do not know of what you speak. This is a respectable woods with no mischief-

causing witches within."

Leah wanted to applaud him. He hid his fear and thoughts well. The ominous figure turned on her so fast she stumbled back a step, but she reminded herself of the tenets of mental protection. She calculated angles in her head as she watched the man walk toward her.

"Do you think to fool me with your deceitful ways and wiles?" He loomed over her.

Still trying to keep the equation in her head, she managed to answer. "Oh, no, sir. I have no deceitful ways or wiles. I'm a simple girl. Pray, how may I be of service?" She made a little curtsey.

The figure transformed back into the now-familiar man. "Simon, good job, though thinking about how crooked the miller is might not be your best safe thought."

Turning to Leah, he smiled. "The geometry was an inspired thought. It would be enough to cause most mind-sweepers to doubt their own thoughts. That curtsey at the end was a bit too much. It would be the equivalent of giving Lionel the middle finger, and you don't want to do that."

"The middle finger. What does that mean?" Simon asked, but a firm nod from her grandfather ended the discussion.

The voices outside grew louder and more agitated. Taking a final peek out the window, he cast a measuring look in her direction. "Granddaughter, you're about as ready as you're going to be. Besides, we have less than two days to make it happen, if my calculations are correct. You must remember two things. Keep in mind to hold yourself proud. They will be more afraid of you than you're of them. By now, your legend has grown."

Leah protested, "I haven't done anything."

"By now," Simon added, "there will be tales of how you transformed into a fire-breathing monster and burned down entire towns."

Would it be to her advantage to encourage the tales? She decided she'd stay silent on the matter. It would be better for people to be unsure. "What is the second thing, Grandfather?"

"Love. There's the love of everyone holding you in his or her intentions. There's the love of Lionel and Arabella. I will always believe love is the ultimate magick." He stood near the door, but motioned the two of them closer.

Laying his hand on Leah's head, he urged Simon to do likewise. Even Esme stuck her cold nose in her hand. Grandfather's deep, resonant voice started. "I bless you in the name of the Lady and the Lord."

Simon's voice joined in, cracking a little. "Spirits, good and kind, go with Leah."

In unison, they spoke, "Elements Air, Fire, Water, and Earth assist Leah in her endeavors."

Her grandfather's voice thickened with emotion. "Woodland creatures, birds in flight, fish in the water, guide your sister home."

Esme barked, adding her own benediction to the blessing. It was time to go. She put her hand on the door.

Grandfather placed a hand on her shoulder. "I cannot go with you. How I wish I could, but Simon can go."

"I can?" His voice cracked on the question.

"Not as you, but as a stately escort. I think a pure-white falcon might do the trick." Waving his hands once more, he turned the open-mouthed Simon into a beautiful white bird. Leah lifted the falcon to her shoulder.

Esme gave three sharp barks.

Grandfather looked down at the dog. "I don't know, Esme, you really are too old for adventures."

The dog looked up at the falcon and barked again.

"Leah, Esme wants to go with you. As an old dog, this may be her last adventure, since she can't return with me. It's fitting she should go in style." He waved his hands once more, transforming the elderly dog into a large black panther with a jeweled collar.

The bird jumped around on her shoulder, squawking. Most people might think it was afraid of the panther, but Leah knew better. Simon was mad he didn't get to be the panther.

"Be at peace, Simon. You're the only one who can fly." Grandfather's words settled the bird some.

Leah turned to the door once more, steeling herself for her upcoming mission.

"One more thing." Grandfather darted to a dark corner and returned with a staff adorned with a rounded crystal sphere on top. He blew on the clear crystal, causing smoke to develop inside. It would seethe one way, then the other, forming images and shapes as it moved. "The ultimate parlor trick, it will, as you say in your time, freak them out." He laughed with delight.

Leah vowed to be brave as she used her staff to counterbalance herself. Simon didn't weigh too much, and the robe protected her from his talons. Her attitude would be similar to that of a mean girl. She'd show no fear and would expect everyone to do her bidding. Esme walked along beside her, soft-footed and menacing.

CHAPTER FIFTEEN

*D*ESPITE THE OPEN *door, none of the knights turned toward her. Peasants ran through the brush, calling out to the knights. The entire yard must be enchanted. As she strolled slowly toward the gate, she put her shoulders back and her chin up, trying to resemble some of the ancient queens she'd seen depicted on temple walls. This was the exam that she'd been preparing for all her life. She swung open the garden gate, attracting attention.*

The first knight removed his helmet and ogled her openly, until Esme growled, drawing his attention downward. "By St. Bartholomew's bones," he cursed, backing up his horse.

The other two knights turned. It was impossible to judge their expressions with their visors down, but their horses expressed their attitude clearly enough by side-stepping and pulling at the reins. It was time to take charge of the situation. It was like a mental order. She hadn't have been surprised if it had come from her grandfather.

Projecting her voice as she'd learned to do in choir, she told them, "You appear to be an adequate escort to take me to my beloved Lionel."

The three knights looked at each other as if confused by her words. "Do not give them time to think." She knew where that order came from. "Knights, where is my mount?" she demanded, stamping her staff to make her petulance more real. She didn't expect the lightning bolt shooting from the crystal. It was hard to tell who was more surprised, Simon flapping his wings wildly from his perch, the knights, or the peasants fleeing into the woods.

A white mare appeared in the clearing with a jeweled bridle and saddle. The white mare approached her and bowed down on its forelegs so she could mount. Thank goodness, for the trail rides in the park that Stella had insisted they do. She'd make a point of thanking her when she arrived home. Inclining her head a mere inch, she said, "This mount is adequate," but her attitude said just only.

Her horse followed behind the knights with showy steps, while Esme stayed close by. Her staff proved problematic as she swung it around, trying to figure out how to ride with it, causing the knights to knee their horses to get out of her way. Eventually, she rested it against her thighs.

News of the slow-moving caravan must have reached people's ears. They peeked through doors and windows and climbed to rooftops to spy. Leah kept her head up. She was no fearful peasant. She was the Queen, the Beloved. She smiled, thinking how right the words felt. Who knew she'd her own inner mean girl to tap into? She certainly hadn't. When she got back, she might have to be nice to Cerberus. Nope, that was just crazy talk.

Hadn't she made this trip before? Hadn't she been half dazed by pain? Before she could mentally revisit those memories, a familiar voice spoke in her head. "Act as you want to be perceived. It was quite common for people to taunt those charged with witchcraft, rather like kicking someone when they were down."

A boy hid by a tree with a rock in his hand. Did he think he'd throw that at her or Esme? Simon lifted off from her shoulder and flew in the direction of the boy, who dropped his rock and fled. Simon circled the area and managed to scare out a few more people with rocks.

As they ran past, Leah looked at them, causing the women to scream and pull their aprons over their faces. What did these people believe that caused so much fear? It had to be something horrible to rationalize killing their neighbors and friends in horrific ways, all in the name of religion.

Miss Santiago had quoted some poem in class about a man in Nazi Germany. It was something about the man not saying anything when they took the Jews, because he wasn't one. Then the Nazis rounded up more groups, until when they finally came for him, there was no one left to stand up for him. Were the people so unaware that this was only another genocide operation? Their time would come. There would be no one to speak for them.

It was her time to stand up. They entered the courtyard of a long, block building. A burly man dressed in leather pants and vest approached her. A chill started up her spine–her torturer. He made a motion for her to dismount. "Do not dismount. You will be at a disadvantage." *This time she didn't need orders. She knew getting off the horse would have been bad. She certainly hoped her mount wasn't Horace the snake.*

People began to slide through the open gates to watch the proceedings. The torturer gestured back to her, making her wonder if he were a mute or a victim of torture who'd had his tongue cut out. You'd think, if so, he'd have been more merciful, but most bullies were misguided, torturing the weak, not necessarily the deserving.

The knights pretended not to notice his gesturing. She wasn't sure if they were mocking the man or unsure how to handle the situation. A young priest hurried out, spoke to the knights, who gestured in her direction, then spurred their mounts and left in a cloud of dust.

"Wait," he called after them, but they did not hear, or they pretended not to.

The priest looked from her to the man in leather, who shrugged his shoulders.

It was past time to move this along, and she knew that this meeting should take place outside so all could witness it. "Tell my beloved Lionel I await his pleasure." *This caused some people in the crowd to titter. Most could remember the friendship between Arabella and Lionel. Some whispered she might have regarded herself well before, but now she was the bloody Queen of England.*

The priest shuffled his feet and gestured to the open door behind him. "Come inside. Your beloved, I mean, Father Lionel waits."

"No." She only said that one word and regarded the priest as if he were joking. Her hands tightened around her staff, and she attempted to bring it upright. Simon lifted from her shoulder as if he didn't trust the staff in her hand. Esme took the opportunity to growl. The crowd grew uneasy, backing up.

Lionel ran out of the building with his black robe flapping behind him. "What farce is this, Arabella?" The thin priest stumbled to an immediate halt, the words stopping as he took in the princely outfitted steed and the jeweled collar on the panther. He walked slowly around the three, making Leah turn her mount to keep him in sight. She didn't trust the man, even if Arabella loved him now or had loved him in the past. Leah Carpenter knew a snake when she saw one. Placing her hand on her steed's neck, she muttered a mental apology just in case her steed was Horace.

"No farce." She smiled. "I came to see my beloved." The men and women jostled each other to see if someone else had entered the area.

Lionel put a cupped hand to his forehead and pretended to look in all directions. "The devil must be hiding. He can't stand to be inside the church walls. I'm surprised you haven't burst into flames."

"Hate to ruin your theory. I hear there's a whole lot more evil inside the walls than there's outside. Who needs the devil when you have the good abbot who enslaves you with drugs and makes up tales using his magick divination bowl? The bowl is not exactly honest, either. Remember when he showed you a picture of me with another man?"

The crowd whispered as Lionel looked down at his hands. His head snapped up. "You must be a witch. No one was in that room except the abbot and me."

Inhaling slowly, she considered her reply. It was time to come out of the broom closet in a very big way. "I never said I wasn't a witch. I said what you saw was a lie. The abbot used magick for evil purposes. I was only twelve when I supposedly played you false."

Lionel held his hands over his ears, shouting, "Get behind me, devil."

If only she'd Arabella's memories. She turned to the crowd, "What was I doing when I was twelve? Did I take off with some bearded courtier?" She'd her fingers crossed, just in case she'd been a bit of a hussy. There was some chattering, but only one woman chose to come forth. "Your twelfth year was when your mother fell from the roof and broke her leg. She was mending the roof your father should have."

The woman earned jeers from the men, while the women hooted in agreement.

"I took care of my mother." She hoped that was the right answer.

"Not only that," the woman continued, "you repaired the roof and helped me with my brood when they fell sick. No longer did you think yourself better than others. You had no interest in marriage or boys. Some thought you were holding out for something better than the men in our village, but I knew the only man you cared for had left town." The woman looked pointedly at Lionel.

Nodding her head at the woman, she said, "Thank you." What was her name? It would have been nice to know the woman who'd chosen to champion Arabella.

"Agnes. My name is Agnes. I did not expect you to remember it since you moved away with your husband three winters ago."

Arabella was married. She'd left town. Maybe Arabella had found some happiness, but this man, this sick, sick man, was determined to snatch it away from her.

"Well," Lionel's voice took on a sneering quality, "it looks like the wages of sin pay well." He crossed his arms in front of him and rocked back on his heels as if he'd said something cleverer than a platitude repeated from countless pulpits.

"I'm not sure to what you refer." She wrestled the staff into an upright position over her burgeoning stomach. Where had that come from? Grandfather had warned her.

He looked pointedly at her stomach. At least she knew she was married, as opposed to being a rape victim, which was somewhat encouraging. Arabella had a chance at a decent life if she could just stay alive, the both of them. Of course, declaring herself hadn't earned her any brownie points.

"Lionel, I wish for a moment you could hear yourself spouting these ridiculous platitudes. When you were a boy, you had a wonderful mind. You wanted to know the why behind things, and I loved you dearly. Now, you're a mindless cog in the church, striking fear into the people with your talk of demons and hell, squeezing them for tithes when they can barely feed their own families. You pretend to forgive their sins when yours are so much blacker."

Lionel darted forward, as if to pull her off the horse. Esme growled, while Simon dived at his head, forcing Lionel to cover it with his hands. "Witch, baby killer, blood drinker," he shouted from behind the shield of his bent arms.

She looked around at the crowd. Holding her staff, she waved it in a circular fashion, causing little spirals of dirt and leaves to lift off the ground. "Do you believe this?" A few shook their heads. Others nodded. Most managed to not move at all.

Looking at Lionel, she asked, "Do you believe this nonsense? After all, your church made it up, preached it from the pulpit, and printed the pamphlets. They had to use images since most people couldn't read."

One man volunteered in the crowd. "I saw one. The witch rode a broomstick across the sky." People crowded around him, asking about the drawings.

Simon returned to her shoulder, which allowed Lionel to lower his arms.

"If you're so smart, Arabella, as you always imagined yourself, why would the church do such a thing? Be careful. If you lie, you might be struck down by lightning." He gave her a sly grin, declaring himself positive he'd outfoxed her.

She smiled, looked back at the crowd, swarming the pamphlet viewer. They needed to hear what she'd to say. It was as much for them as it was for Lionel. She shook her staff, wondering if she could get a lightning bolt out of it. Instead, fireworks burst into the sky, from Roman candles to pinwheels and bees buzzing across the courtyard. The crowd gasped, oohed and aahed, and eventually laughed at their initial fright.

"Very pretty," Lionel commented, lifting an eyebrow. "Is that your answer? I expected as much from you."

Leah would have liked lightning, but she'd to admit she'd the crowd's attention now. "I came back for you, Lionel, because I cared about what you were being turned into with the drugs, the lies, and the witch hunts."

Lionel started to speak, but she held her hand up. "I'm not finished. You asked me why the church started these witch hunts. Number one, they want to wipe out all competing religions. They want to get rid of all worship of other deities. They cannot control people or their money if They're not part of the same faith. They also cannot allow those who practice the old ways to live. They're wrong. I come from a place where many religions exist side by side. It isn't a perfect place, but people are free to practice their various faiths without fear of torture or death."

One woman yelled out, "I thought your husband's people were in the next village."

"Farther than that," was as much Leah was willing to commit to. She wondered why they only saw Arabella and not Leah. "More important," she projected her voice, "the witch hunts are to frighten you. First, they make up the evil blood drinkers that only the church can get rid of for a price. Convenient, when no such people exist. If you ever say anything against the church, they can call you a heretic, threaten to send your eternal soul to hell, and torture you in this world. Don't forget, they want your money and your land, too."

The mob, swayed by the emotional images, began to gripe about the greedy church and bloodsucking priests stealing their immortal souls and their gold. The crowd seemed to change its tune. In fact, it might have been a great time to leave if Leah had had a clue which way to go. The sounds of a rowdy crowd were familiar enough to her. At least this time, they didn't have pitchforks or flaming torches.

A short, bald man slipped out the side door, carrying a cauldron. A sudden memory flash alerted her that she was in the presence of the black abbot, the clergyman who didn't care who he hurt or killed in his quest for money and power. Grandfather had described him as a bad one. The fireworks and a large cat with a jeweled collar were enough to impress the crowd. Who knew what this man might do?

No one else noticed him. He put down the cauldron, waved his hands over it, commanding it. Lionel was yelling something. The crowd jeered him, but no one noticed the black ooze taking form above the pot. It resembled some type of twisted creature with wings. He was shaping it for her, that she knew. Think ahead. Was there any firepower left in the staff? She certainly hoped so.

Mesmerized by the black, oily creature, Leah was afraid to look away. The second she looked away, it would attack. The sun must have slipped behind the clouds. The sky grew dark, taking a bright sunny day into dusk in a few seconds. The sounds of wings flapping behind her came nearer. It was an illusion to distract her into turning away. It wouldn't work. She'd be ready when the dark creature sprang at her.

The screams in the background vaguely registered, along with Simon's squeezing talons. The boy didn't do bird impersonations well. The abbot's smug smile crumpled before he screamed as a river of fire hit him and his *creature, igniting them both. Looking upward, she saw the silhouette of a huge golden dragon. Simon danced up and down her arm in agitation, which meant the dragon had to be her grandfather. Why was he here? He might miss going back in time.*

His voice spoke clearly in her head. "I had to, Granddaughter. I saw the black abbot was up to no good. Only a ceremonial magician can deal with that type of evil. Let's head back to the portal. I'll show you the way."

Holding the left rein tight, she turned the mare in a circle. Lionel stood near the smoking mess consisting of what was left of his mentor and his creation. Perhaps he'dn't learned anything. Then again, some of the people in the village might have. They might hesitate to start up another witch hunt again. Arabella would live after she'd her child.

Leah urged her mount after the golden dragon. The panther ran beside her while Simon flew overhead.

People actually cheered them as she rode. It was a little different from her earlier trip through town. Golden dragons had a way of reminding people that magick was afoot, even when they'd forgotten it.

She could see the cabin through the trees, shimmering, changing, and hard to see. The portal was open. She didn't have much time. The shadow of the dragon hovered over the portal, as opposed to landing. Grandfather was waiting for her. Digging her heels into her mount, she urged it faster, but her mount changed underneath her legs. Her white coat became brown and rough. Her beautiful, elegant head had huge horns. Her beautiful saddle disappeared, causing her to fall. Using the staff, she stopped her fall. She held herself up for a minute, watching the house in front of her blink in and out of existence. Her legs started running before she'd even formed a coherent thought. Her large pregnant belly slowed her down. Wrapping her arms around it, she sprinted for the gate. She made it inside the gate just as Grandfather changed to stand beside her. Outside the fence, Simon turned back into a teen, holding up the staff she'd dropped. Esme stood beside him, along with a beautiful, dark-haired woman who was obviously pregnant. Leah placed a hand on her flat stomach just as everything began to spin. There was a sense of movement and colors shifting that went on forever, only to end with them ejected as if out of a water slide.

Instead of being in a shallow pool, they found themselves in the back alley of a strip mall Laundromat that blew warm dryer-sheet-scented air on them.

Leah wondered if everyone who used the Laundromat always brought dryer sheets. *Dryer sheets?* That meant she was home. Her hand clutched her grandfather's hand. His expression remained shuttered. Leah hoped he made it through the portal okay since he was no longer young.

Not opening his eyes, he said, "Use your barriers, child. There are some things I'd rather not hear."

Good. Still alive. Barriers, she'd set them up. The area looked unfamiliar. Nudging her grandfather, she asked, "Do you know where we're?"

What if they'd showed up in the wrong country or century? They'd taken a right at that last portal when they should have taken a left. His eyes fluttered open. "Can you give me a minute? I want to appreciate things for the last twenty years I've been imagining. I don't want to rush it. Think my calculations may have been off by a day."

Leah stood still, holding her grandfather's hand and tried to pull him into a seated position. "I noticed. You may not want to hurry, but I do. I can't wait to shower off the smell of roasted human flesh. We need to hoof it home before the police pick us up."

"Okay," Grandfather agreed, as he struggled to stand. "I don't remember standing being this hard. Do you think I aged while traveling through time? Like a thousand years?"

"Not a thousand, but a good five hundred," she teased. She certainly felt years older than the girl who'd lived in fear of Cerberus. Once you met real evil face to face, mean girls were a poor second.

Pointing to the strip mall, he suggested, "We can go inside and use a phone and get a ride home?"

She couldn't see anyone letting them use their cell, but someone might. Wait, her grandfather had meant a public phone. Did they have those anymore? They rounded the Laundromat to see a bar that offered a blue-plate lunch special.

"The Red Rooster. Charlie's place." His pace quickened as he approached.

Instead of explaining that she wasn't allowed in the bar, she simply followed. The place was almost empty except for a woman contemplating a jukebox, while a bald man wiped down the bar. Grandfather stared at the man intently. "You're Charlie's son."

"Yep," the man agreed. "So who might you be? Already dressed up for Halloween?"

She watched her grandfather open and close his mouth without saying anything, upset that he wasn't recognized. Stepping up to the bar, she winked at the man. "Surely, you recognize Buell Hare, the man who disappeared off the face of the earth, say, about twenty years ago."

The man leaned forward his expression avid. "Yes, I remember that tale. My dad came up with some outlandish tale about you disappearing in time. Did you?"

"I'm not allowed to say," Grandfather said with a smile. "Can I use your phone?"

The bartender pulled a desk phone from under the bar and placed it on the slick counter. Leah reached for the phone. "Let me call. I know the number, and they were kinda expecting me back, so it won't be as big of a shock."

CHAPTER SIXTEEN

T HE PHONE RANG once before a breathless voice answered. "Hello?"

Leah wasn't sure if it was her mother or her sister. They both sounded similar, especially with the slight edge of hysteria coloring the one word, both anxious to hear news but frightened, too. Thank the Goddess she'd made it back in one piece. Her family had suffered by not knowing what had happened in the past and being helpless to assist. It was better this way. No doubt, Nana would have opened a can of whoop-ass on the abbot. The thought made her giggle.

"I do not have time for prank phone calls," her mother practically shouted in her ear.

Oh yeah, she'd forgotten to say something. "Mom, it's me. I'm back."

"Leah, sweetheart, is that you?" Her voice trembled with uncertainty and a quiver of hope.

"Yes, of course." She tried to put all the love and affection in her voice she'd denied her mother the past couple of years. Suddenly, all her teen angst fell way. She'd always thought her parents never understood. Maybe they did understand. Who knew what shadows, and possibly dragons, their pasts held?

"Are you here?" Laughter followed her inquiry. "I'm just being silly now. No way could you call over the centuries." Her voice grew higher and lighter, losing the doubt.

"Mom, can Dad pick me up? I'm at a bar called the Red Rooster."

Leah twisted around to see where her grandfather was. He stood in front of the old-time jukebox, peering into it.

"Never heard of most of these people," he grumbled. The bartender ignored him and continued polishing glasses.

The smell of stale smoke caused her to cough and miss her mother's reply. "What?"

"I said we will all come. Me, your father, Nana, and Ethan, since he's small. Nora won't like being left out, but I imagine she can wait." Her mother continued to babble.

"Wait, Mom. Are you listening?" Her mother chattered about making her favorite meal, chicken and dumplings. Knowing her mother, she'd eventually run down and get tired of talking.

"Maura, who is on the phone?" Her father's voice came over the line distantly, then more clearly. "Leah, is that you?"

She could hear the smile in his voice. "It's me. I was telling Mom she shouldn't bring everyone, since I brought someone home with me."

The bartender walked over to the jukebox and fed it a couple of quarters, to Grandfather's delight. He began punching buttons wildly, while her father warned her about the dangers of removing someone from another century.

The sound of Frankie Valli and The Four Seasons crooning *Big Girls Don't Cry* filled the empty bar, bouncing off the paneled walls and veneer tables. Grandpa jumped in on the chorus, "Big girls, they don't cry-yi-yi." The bartender snorted his opinion and turned away. The woman who'd been at the jukebox earlier reappeared tying on a white apron.

"Who is that singing?" Leah's father asked.

"Well," Leah hesitated with her explanation, not sure how to put it. "I bet it is someone you've been waiting a long time to meet."

Her father's words came slowly, almost in disbelief. "Is it? Could it be?"

"We could both benefit from a shower and dinner. Ask Nana where the Red Rooster is. Apparently, it used to be one of Grandfather's hangouts."

"Will do. We're leaving now."

"Don't break any speed limits," she teased. "We'ren't going anywhere." The hum of the dial tone told her he'd hung up.

The server turned toward her grandfather, who warbled with gusto. The neon beer signs cast an unflattering glow on her heavily made-up face, emphasizing every wrinkle. Speaking in a smoker's contralto, she asked, "Buell, is that you under all that hair?"

Stopping his impromptu performance, he placed one soft-booted foot behind him and pivoted. "Beverly McClary, still working at the Rooster. Some things never change. Still as pretty as ever."

The woman laughed. "Now I know your eyesight is going." She brushed away the compliment as she gestured with her hand in the air. "What's with the costume? It's not time for trick-or-treating. Even if it was, I'd have to say you're a bit too old."

The bartender slid a soft drink in front of Leah, which she gulped gratefully. Normally, she'd have worried about money, but in the past week, little things such as money, school, and even hygiene had taken second place. As bad as the lingering aroma of cigarettes smelled in the small, dark bar, she knew she herself had to smell worse. A shower was the first thing on her list. Her robe was washable, she hoped.

She savored the cold sweetness against her tongue. On one hand, it had no great nutritional value. It certainly wasn't the same as drinking cool spring water or eating gruel. Although, eating would have been too generous a description for what they'd done with the gruel. That would imply it had had a chewable texture. At best, they'd consumed it.

Leah watched her grandfather talk to the waitress with obvious relish after twenty-plus years with no one to talk to, except for the travelers he'd willed to step in his direction. None of them would remember him as Buell Hare. The villagers would recall seeing only a magnificent golden dragon, or would they?

Draining the last of her drink, she refused the offer of a refill. No reason to fill up on a soda when she'd have real food in a few minutes. Had she done what she was supposed to do? It felt like she'd, and she felt a sense of completion. What had she done, really?

The fact that Arabella had already married and expected a baby made it seem like she hadn't really needed Leah's help. That was true, up to a point. Lionel might still have executed her as a witch after she'd had the baby. Grandfather had done a spectacular job of ridding the world of a singularly malevolent force, in turn preventing more torture and the deaths of suspected witches.

If her destiny hadn't been to go back in time, Grandfather wouldn't have been there. Bev, the waitress, teased her grandfather about looking like a cross between Santa Claus and an elderly Friar Tuck. Hard to imagine him as a fire-breathing dragon, but when it came to family, he protected his.

Was that it? Had she done anything? Had she changed Lionel's beliefs? No doubt, he'd have changed on his own without his regular drug supply and the abbot whispering evil lies into his drug-addled mind. The changes would start with Lionel. If not him, there was always Simon. Even if only a couple of the villagers changed their minds, it would be a start.

Most would go back to the old ways of thinking, because that was easier. The girl on the beautiful white mare, with the sleek panther and snow-white falcon, was a dream, a lie, a story told to confuse good Christians. As for the golden dragon, they would assure each other saying that dragons don't exist. They'd probably forget about the abbot, too. If they did remember his evil ways, they would question what happened.

As she slowly turned her empty glass around on the bar, spreading the condensation across the surface, a strange thought entered her head. Would history remember them? A quote Miss Santiago had attributed to Napoleon was that winners always wrote history. They could justify any horrific behavior or choose not to mention it. Were they the winners?

THE DOOR OPENED, letting in the strong afternoon sun as her father, mother, and Nana pushed in at the same time. For a second, she was sure they'd get stuck in the door. Mother stumbled in first, blinking in the sudden dimness, but finally spotting Leah, she darted toward her.

"My baby girl," she cooed, wrapping her arms around her. Her mother pulled away slightly and wrinkled her nose. "Pew, what is that smell?"

"Trust me, you don't want to know." She rested her head on her mother's shoulder. The incongruity of having a family reunion at the local neighborhood dive was lost on her mother. Her father stood off to the side, waiting his turn, while Nana walked hesitantly into the center of the room, staring at the back of her grandfather, who slowly turned.

"Buell." Her voice was little more than a whisper but carried across the room.

He started toward her in a walk but jogged the last two steps and swept her up in an embrace that lifted her feet from the ground. Leah backhanded her eyes, suddenly tear-filled, and her mother did the same.

"My Esmeralda, my sweet girl. How I missed you." He gently lowered her feet to the floor, landing a kiss on her hair.

"I missed you, too," Nana confessed in a soft voice that Leah didn't recognize.

Her father drifted over to her and wrapped an arm around her. "I'm glad you're back, Trinka."

She leaned against her father, realizing this was as probably as emotional as he got. "Me, too. I even learned something."

"Oh, really?" her father replied, giving her shoulders a little squeeze. "Anything I might want to hear?"

Whenever something went wrong, instead of scolding her or placing blame, her father would ask her what she'd learned from the incident. The familiarity of the routine comforted her.

SIGHING, SHE RUBBED her hand over her face. "I appreciate my family more than I ever did. I also think I understand why the desire to have power over others is so incredibly dangerous. It should make you wonder about anyone in a powerful position or office."

The bartender snorted his agreement, while her father motioned for her to continue.

"People accept scary stories even when they're made up because someone they believe to be smarter than They're relayed the information."

Her father's lips tugged upward into a smile. "Sweetheart, right now you know more than about eighty percent of the world. Anything else you care to elaborate on? Sounds to me like you had an eye-opening trip."

Eye-opening, yeah, she might call it that, or deadly, or transformative. "What can I say, Dad? It was something. Something I never want to repeat again." She laughed more out of relief than anything else.

"Thanks for the drink." She turned to go, wondering why neither of her parents had mentioned her sitting at a bar. Nana had her hand tucked into her husband's arm and her head held close to his, talking animatedly. She suspected they were exchanging sweet nothings. When she drew closer, she overheard their conversation.

"Goddess help me, Buell. There's no one I love more than you, but if you ever think of leaving me again, there's no place far enough that you'll be able to hide from my wrath."

Grandfather's voice held a bit of humor. "Ah, darling, there's no place I want to be but by your side."

Leah grinned as she climbed into the backseat of the car. Finally, she was getting to know her grandfather. Not only was he an incredible ceremonial magician, but it looked like he was a charmer, too. He'd the gift of charisma, which would be a beneficial gift to have.

Working her back into the cushioned seat, she sighed and closed her eyes. So much she'd missed about her century. Anything well cushioned was one of them.

Her mother twisted her body to peer into the backseat. "While you were gone, you had a visitor."

Who could that be? Especially since Stella knew she was gone.

Her mother's expression turned playful. "An attractive fellow named Dylan."

"Dylan? Dylan came by. Um, you didn't tell him I was out of the century did you?" Odd things sometimes happened in her family, but crossing centuries might have been even more difficult.

Her mother's laughter filled the car. "Of course not. I mentioned you were too sick for visitors. I'm not sure if he believed me. He left a card and the cutest stuffed animal, a dragon."

Grandfather quipped, "The boy has taste. Dragons are so much better than silly teddy bears."

Dylan had come by and brought her a gift. That was a very good sign. Her certainty about what a perfect boyfriend he'd be began to shimmer in her mind, like the portal had before it had blinked out of existence. Then again, she almost hadn't made it back here. Why not see what he'd to say in his card before deciding on a happily ever after ending?

CHAPTER SEVENTEEN

NORA AND ETHAN ran out of the house before the car had even stopped. They danced around her, trying to push each other out of the way to hug her. Even Theodora, her cat, got in on the action by weaving through their legs, almost tripping her. Ethan was the first to step back, shaking his head. "Whoo wee, you stink."

She wrinkled her nose at her brother's comment, knowing it was true. Her charmed gown apparently did not keep her fresh smelling. Its abilities included keeping her alive and bringing her back, which it had done very well.

Both Nora and Ethan stared at the man exiting the car from the other door. Their expressions mirrored surprise and curiosity. Of course, neither had ever met their grandfather.

He turned to face his staring grandchildren. His eyes twinkled as he held his arms wide. "There are the rest of my grandchildren. Come here."

Ethan readily hurled himself into the man's waiting arms with an enthusiastic, "Grandpa!"

Nora hung back a bit, biting her lip, looking a trifle uncertain. Grandfather managed to smile at Nora over Ethan's head. "No worries. I'm real, not like the dreams you've had."

Nora's hand flew up to cover her gasp. "How did you know about my dreams?" Her feet moved her closer, even if she didn't seem to be aware of her actions.

"You told me yourself." Grandpa tapped his forehead. He winked at Leah and mentally reminded her of the importance of barriers. "You practically shouted that you've seen me in your dreams, which demonstrates your exceptional psychic abilities. I've been trying to communicate with the family."

Nora nodded vigorously. Ethan released Grandfather's waist, giving him a thorough scrutiny. "You stink, too, but not as bad as Leah."

Reaching his gnarled hand out, he mussed Ethan's hair. "The ability to speak one's thoughts without fear of condemnation is a magnificent blessing. I congratulate you, Ethan. My hygiene may have suffered from living alone too much. I will do my best to improve. I'm sure your grandmother will encourage me." Everyone laughed, as he'd intended.

He nodded in Leah's direction. "I will yield the shower to you since you're in the greatest need."

Actually, she'd have preferred to read Dylan's card first, but she could do that in the bathroom, since her family overwhelmingly agreed she smelled foul. At least in the bathroom, she hadn't have to worry about anyone reading over her shoulder.

Their noisy reunion attracted some gawkers among the neighbors. The widow, who lived closest to them, muttered to herself, loud enough for them to hear. "Dressed up for Halloween. They're all a bit odd. At least they keep their lawn cut."

Leah followed behind Nora and her grandfather, who were in deep discussion about her dreams. Ethan worked his hand into hers, surprising her a little. She squeezed his hand, hoping she managed to convey how glad she was to be back.

"I understand that." Nora's voice drifted back to her. "Still, there's this man who I'm sure is calling me from the past. Some nights when I close my eyes, he's there."

Ethan and Leah looked at each other.

Grandfather patted Nora's hand. "Sounds like we need to talk."

Ethan stood on his tiptoes to whisper in Leah's ear. "Looks like someone else is getting ready to have an adventure."

I hope not, she wanted to add, but chose to say nothing. Instead, she contemplated the smooth cap of hair covering Nora's head, a modern cut belonging to a practical woman, not someone who would enjoy the past. It wasn't as if she'd liked her experience, but then, she'd learned from it.

The aroma of chicken and dumplings wafted outside from the open kitchen door. Lifting her nose, she inhaled greedily. Better get the showering done. She could tuck into the food, but first she'd like to see the card and the dragon. As if sensing her thoughts, her mother handed over the card and small stuffed animal as soon as she cleared the doorway.

She flourished the dragon. "Look! It's golden."

Grandfather, understanding her reason in mentioning the color, grinned. "I don't even know the boy, but already I like him. Of course, he'll have to go through me before dating one of my granddaughters."

Her father cleared his throat, noisily, threw back his shoulders and puffed out his chest, she assumed in an effort to appear larger. "Buell, you'll have your turn after me."

Rolling her eyes, she headed to her room to grab some clean clothes before heading to the shower. If either of them were serious, she doubted she'd ever go out. Her father would quiz her date on the three basic laws of Newtonian physics and the Pythagorean Theorem. Her grandfather was a different story. It was hard to be sure what he would do, especially after he scanned her date's mind.

No wonder her mother had waited until college to seriously date. Her mother had mentioned something about her father disappearing shortly after she'd met Adam, her soon-to-be husband. No wonder he'd managed to date Mom. She suspected grandfather could be intimidating when he wanted to be.

She stood at the bathroom door and yelled, "Going in. Does anyone need to use the bathroom first?"

Ethan darted in front of her, giving a curious look to her armful of supplies. She waited, wondering why she'd said anything, but it was common courtesy when you had one bathroom. A few minutes' wait was a very small price to pay for running water and a flush toilet. The thought of a toothbrush with actual toothpaste excited her.

The sound of flushing accompanied Ethan opening the door. He glanced at the dragon again, but surprisingly said nothing, very unlike him. Was she getting a reprieve from his usual comments due to her recent absences? More likely, their parents had threatened to take away his dance video game. Most boys favored games containing mayhem, destruction, and death. The game manufacturers labeled the games with either patriotic or sexy names to fool indulgent parents.

After finishing her own real-life game in which she'd been the dreaded enemy, she found the idea of the single-player role-playing game repulsive. Music began to pulsate from the living room. Ethan was probably showing Grandfather his moves. The clatter of dishes in the kitchen signaled dinner loomed ever closer.

The bathroom door shut, she turned on the shower, giving it time to warm up. Using her index finger, she slid it under the flap of the barely sealed envelope. Still, it remained sealed, which proved no one had read it. Nana could have just rested it against her forehead, but she doubted she had.

The card featured a cartoon pair of animals with one tucked up in bed with an ice pack on its head. The card inscription read: Hope You're Back on Your Feet Soon. Underneath it, Dylan had carefully written in slanting letters, *I miss you. Geometry class has become even more boring, if that's possible. Can't wait to see you. Dylan.*

He couldn't wait to see her. Leah held the card to her chest and then read it again. She was tempted to read it once more, but that might cut into her hot-water time. She placed the card inside the vanity cabinet so an errant splash wouldn't smear the sentiment.

The warm water pelted her, both stinging and reviving her. A soapy loofah rid her body of all dirt and odor not belonging to the twenty-first century. Her body was soon red from the scrubbing and felt oddly vulnerable.

People tended to take showers naked, so that wasn't it. She was missing her magickal covering. Pulling the curtain back, she peeked at the robe wadded in the corner. It didn't appear too enchanted any longer, just dirty and wrinkled. Could it be she'd used up all the power? Maybe it had disappeared when she no longer needed it. Often, at the end of rituals, they grounded the energy, sending it back into the earth. Maybe in removing the robe, she'd grounded the magick. It made sense.

For the first time in her life, she shampooed her hair twice, as the directions stated, before using conditioner. Her mother's response to the directions was that they only said that so the manufacturer could make more money. Her mother was right, but she'd to get the smoke smell out of her hair.

She lifted her hair to the shower spray, thinking how light she felt. Her arms lifted so easily. Who knew magick had actual physical weight? If she dealt with it all the time, like Grandfather or Nana, she might become more accustomed to it. Now, it was gone, and she missed it. It seemed like the equivalent of snapping off a finger or a toe. Make that, three fingers and a toe.

A hammering at the door stooped her musing.

"Dinner's on"

Not too much had changed in the few days she'd been gone. Meals waited for no one in her family. Sliding clothes over her still-damp body proved difficult but not impossible. She wrapped her long hair in a towel turban. Looking at the cabinet, she debated taking her card. She plucked her card off the top of the toiletries. If she left it, someone might actually knock something over on to it.

A stop at her room allowed Leah to place the card and dragon on her dresser. Theodora, perched on her bed, thrashed her tail, expressing discontent that Leah didn't trust her. That was Leah's interpretation, though. She was unsure her pet wouldn't investigate her dresser. She opened a drawer and dropped the card and dragon inside.

Dinner was a noisy affair with everyone asking her questions about Arabella and Lionel. Grandfather regaled everyone with his impressions of various folks. Leah decided not to mention he'd never left his portal cabin until the last day. Before the meal was up, she found herself yawning.

"Off to bed with you, young lady," her mother urged.

After hugging everyone once more, she stumbled off to her room, excited at the idea of slipping between clean sheets. With her door ajar, she heard her mother speaking to her father as she combed the tangles out of her hair.

"Adam, I'm not sure if sending her right back to school is such a good idea. She may need a debriefing of sorts or at least time to recover."

Leah swung her door back open. "I'm going to school. I missed enough days already. It is what I want, and it will help me to get back to normal."

Her mother's face reflected surprise, while her father agreed with her. "Sounds like the right thing to do."

With another disaster averted, she was ready to sink into a deep, dreamless sleep, but she didn't. Instead, she visited the village she'd so recently left, but instead of being a person, she felt more like a hovering presence, rather cloud-like.

The village hummed with the sound of an anvil ringing, the bleating of goats, people chattering, and the thud of wagon wheels and horses' hooves.

A wagon came into view with a couple setting on the bench seat. The dark-haired woman rocked a small bundle. The man wore a floppy hat that shadowed half his face.

"I not thought to come back here," the woman commented.

Leah immediately recognized Arabella's voice. She tried to peer under the hat shadow to get a glance at her mysterious husband with no luck. Clouds, if that's what she was, were not that maneuverable. She drifted along with the wagon, listening to the conversation.

"The only decent thing is to thank Agnes for her interference and creative lies," the man commented.

She'd heard that voice before. It sounded different, though, deeper.

Arabella held the baby up to her shoulder, exposing a tiny white face and dark hair. "I would have been lost if Agnes had not come up with the story of my husband and such. It made a decent woman out of me."

The story about Arabella's marriage hadn't been true, then. She'd wondered why grandfather had said Arabella had been raped. This explained it somewhat, but who was the man with her?

"The baby is a mirror image of you," he commented, slowing the horses near a small cottage. Tying off the reins, he descended to help Arabella and child alight. The woman from the crowd appeared in the doorway.

She hurried out to peer at the baby. "Have you chosen a name yet?"

"Yes," Arabella answered. She glanced at the man, who removed his hat, revealing the clean lines of Simon's face. "We named her Leah, after a close friend."

Ah, now everything made sense. Simon removed something from the wagon as Agnes asked Arabella, "Have you heard the news of your old neighbor Lionel?"

"I haven't" Arabella answered while fussing over the baby. She held up the child, who was dressed in an elaborate gown.

"Not long after you left with the dragon and oversized cat, his heart failed him. Some say it was the devil taking his due. I suspect he died from love of you."

"It was more likely the first," Arabella announced. "All the same, his death saddens me. He'd so much potential."

Simon rounded the wagon with a chicken in his arms.

"What is that?" Agnes called out.

Leah thought it was obvious, but it could have been a rhetorical question.

The woman grinned and held out her arms to accept the gift.

Simon gave her the chicken with an admonishment. "This is not a dinner chicken. It is a magickal chicken. You'll always have plenty of eggs and never starve. Never give her away. Never boast about her, or someone will steal her."

Agnes clutched the chicken tightly, causing it to cluck in protest. "I know how folks are around here. Things are good now. People tolerate one another. Before you know it, someone else will turn up threatening brimstone and damnation. Last thing I would do is talk about my magickal hen."

The three nodded in agreement, then looked up in the direction she hovered, almost as if they could feel her presence.

The dream ended as she lay in a state between sleep and total wakefulness, contemplating all she'd heard. It answered her questions. Life was better in the village, at least for a while, according to Agnes. There always seemed to be someone who wanted to rile people up. Sometimes they could do it by promising eternal damnation. Other times, as in now, they just threatened to take away whatever had value. The more things changed, the more they stayed the same.

Her alarm rang, startling her, since she didn't remember setting it.

For a moment, she stayed under the covers, warm and safe, with the sound of Theodora's loud purring in her ear. If she didn't move, her mother wouldn't wake her. She already knew her mother's opinion on going to school today. Though she'd never been a morning person, the thought of Dylan had her vaulting out of bed.

She needed time to get ready to look her best to return to school. Opening her closet to find clean clothes, she thanked the school board members who'd voted for uniforms. Leah was well aware that she might be the only girl who thought it was a wonderful thing. Her hair was clean, which was another plus. If only she could get in the bathroom before Ethan.

The sound of her brother singing killed that hope. Well, she could wash her face in the kitchen and apply her makeup in her room. If she'd to put up with a little brother who hogged the bathroom for acoustics, so be it. In another year, she'd be away at college.

Leah now found even the most mundane things about school thrilling. She even gave Cerberus a big smile, causing Brianna to run into a locker. She reminded her of Sabina, obsessed about her appearance and the need for all boys to notice her. Sabina wasn't that bad, vain, self-absorbed, but she'd good traits, too. Maybe there was some good about Cerberus.

Leah accepted the homework her teachers gave her, although she was tempted to ask how long she'd been gone. That would have made her sound stupid. *Excuse me, but I've been away in another century, and I'm unsure if time progresses the same in both centuries.* Yep, that would probably get her a vacation at the residential facility that a tenth of the school regularly seemed to check into on a rotating basis. Leah believed that had more to do with the parents than the kids. Did the parents have good insurance? Were the parents tired of teenage moodiness and defiance? If so, the facility even had an admissions counselor, who looked a lot like a professional wrestler.

It was almost time for geometry. As much as she wanted to check her appearance, she bypassed the mirror stop to avoid detention. Hurrying to class, she fell in step with Dylan, who turned and stopped.

"You're back," he said, stating the obvious.

"I am," Leah answered in another understatement.

Dylan grinned. "I'm so happy you're okay." The math teacher stood by the door with his arms folded, looking less than impressed in the presence of young love.

"You're both late," he growled the words as a threat, causing the two of them to rush into class.

After geometry, Dylan walked her to English class, where they stood close in the hall, but not touching. Her heart beat as fast as when she'd been sure the oily creature was going to get her. Maybe not that fast, but close enough.

"I was wondering," Dylan started, and then stopped when the English teacher appeared in the door.

The teacher raised one eyebrow, then said, "Believe it or not, Dylan Torres, I, too, was young once. I'm going to write you a pass for your next class. Say what you need to say before I get back. Remember, this is the only pass you'll get from me."

Dylan looked astonished at the idea that Mrs. Barkin had been young once. He gauged her distance before blurting out his invitation. "Leah, would you go out with me this Friday?"

Her heart gave a little jump. Everything was turning out exactly the way she wanted. "I'd love to."

"You would?" Surprise colored his voice. "I mean, I'm glad you would. I know you heard about my father being a minister. I figured that might scare you off."

She heard the sharp heel taps of the teacher. "I'm not afraid."

The teacher appeared with a pass in her hand. "Mr. Torres, make haste to get to class."

Dylan took off in a slight run as Leah entered the classroom, only to have Stella wave at her. She weaved around the desks to sit next to her friend.

Stella hugged her with so much enthusiasm that it caught some of the other students' attention. "Thank goodness, you're back. I've been slaving away on our essay. The good news is I finished it. The bad news is Mrs. Barkin likes it so well she wants us to present it to the class."

Leah collapsed into her chair at the thought of a public presentation, quickly followed by the thought that plenty of people were willing to say stupid, hateful things. Why not try to make a difference for once? She and Stella might wake up a few students to help them realize they'd been guilty of participating in religious stereotyping.

Any female who could face down the abbot could deal with a high school English class. In a flash, Leah realized she could do anything as long as she believed she could.

THE END

If you enjoyed this book, why not sample the entire Pagan Eyes series.

Leah Carpenter thought being the only witch in her local high school was hard. That was until she inexplicably found herself in the past running from an angry mob, which turned out to be much harder. Lionel, the man in charge of the mob, holds a grudge against a girl he calls Arabella. He thinks she's Arabella.

Luckily, just about the time it looks as if she's done for she pops back into her century. This causes trouble at school, but at least she has an understanding family. What happens in the past can hurt her. The whiplashes covering her body are proof enough.

Her Nana believes she has to right a wrong in the past to stay in the present and go out with her crush, Dylan. What she discovers in the past is an evil so pure that it makes her blood run cold. She might not ever make it back to geometry class or more importantly a possible date with Dylan.

Nora Carpenter is a trainee assistant physician, a part-time diner chef… and a witch. Hiding from the memory of a traumatic rape – fueled by prejudice over her eccentric reputation – she keeps herself to herself. Hard work, study, and a cold shoulder to any guy that crosses her path, seem like her best defense.

But when Nora starts having vivid dreams about a compelling, mysterious stranger with dark curls, sexy eyes and a charming Irish lilt, her defenses seem to be breaking. He says he is her soul mate – that he has conquered many centuries to contact her. Can this be real? Or is she going mad? Nora tries to fight the gentle seduction that threatens to thaw her icy façade. But when she's forced to come face to face with real evil she must call on all her magical resources, including her lover from another life, to save her.

Ethan finds himself trapped between the world he knows and the world that could be. A sadistic bully, an unsympathetic principal, and an unreachable love interest make high school difficult for Ethan. He feels like he's living a lie, trying to blend in at school in an effort to keep his head attached to his body.

Fear that he's not the son his father wants negates the support his Wiccan family offers. An impromptu trip into the future saves him from an enraged bully while instilling doubts about where he really belongs. Somehow, he has to find a way to survive in his own world tossing aside his mask and doubts.

AFFIRMATION

RAYNA NOIRE

Stella's college life transforms from sweet to rancid when her boyfriend asks her to do the unthinkable. How did she end up holding her best friend's future in her hands? Anything she does will trigger the disastrous conclusion. If that is not bad enough.

Add in a lunatic minister, a demi-goddess, and a walk through another dimension full of vindictive shrubbery and wildlife. It's a freshman year that she may not survive.

Faerie Lights Series: Glimmer

Available August 2016

Visit www.raynanoire.weebly.com